R. J H. A.

Poems and other verses

R. J H. A.

Poems and other verses

ISBN/EAN: 9783744722735

Printed in Europe, USA, Canada, Australia, Japan

Cover: Foto ©Andreas Hilbeck / pixelio.de

More available books at **www.hansebooks.com**

POEMS

AND OTHER VERSES

H. A. R. J.

"The wind blows east, the wind blows west,
  And there comes good luck and bad ;
  The thriftiest man is the cheerfulest ;
  'Tis a thriftless thing to be sad, sad,
  'Tis a thriftless thing to be sad."

T. FISHER UNWIN

PATERNOSTER SQUARE

CONTENTS.

	PAGE
TO ALTHEA .	I
THE MIGRATION OF THE MUSES	4
FAREWELL .	18
THE PRIVY COUNSELLOR	19
DISAPPOINTMENT .	21
A CHILD'S PLAINT	23
THE SALE OF THE FRENCH CROWN JEWELS	29
FOR A CHRISTMAS CARD .	31
TRANSLATION	32
THE FIRST LOVE-SONG .	34
A JUBILEE SONG .	35
EPITAPH .	38
IN MEMORIAM. A. L. M.	39
DEATH .	41
YOU AND I .	43
A PLAY ON THE LAST MINSTREL	48
PULPIT RHETORIC .	54
TO D. M. J.	55
ORTHOGRAPHY .	58

CONTENTS.

	PAGE
MAGDALEN FANCIES	59
AN AMERICAN TRAGEDY IN A NUT-SHELL	62
"SIGNÔRA WRANGLER"	63
THE SEA-GULL	65
MYSTERIES OF GRACE	67
SONNET	68
ICHABOD	69
CHRISTMAS	71
CHRISTMAS EVE	73
TO THE SWALLOWS	75
TO ALTHEA: A WELCOME	78
TO H. J.: A CHRISTMAS GREETING	79
ARMA VIRUMQUE CANO!	80
A POSTSCRIPT	83
THE DEATH OF THE DUKE OF CLARENCE AND AVONDALE	86
SPERO MELIORA	88
TO MY DOG	93
ON A SWALLOW'S NEST IN THE DOORWAY OF A VILLAGE SCHOOL	98
LINES FOR CHRISTMAS CARDS	101
MATERNAL LOVE	103
YOU'RE ANOTHER	108
A GREETING	109
POETRY	110
THE LOSS OF THE "VICTORIA"	115
"DE AMICITIÂ"	119
ANALOGUE	122

CONTENTS.

PAGE

TO ALL WHOM IT MAY CONCERN 123

ALAS! A LOSS! AND A LASS! 126

SURSUM CORDA . . . 129

NOTA BENE 131

CHRIST IN MODERN THEOLOGY . . 132

PER CRUCEM AD LUCEM . . . 137

A SIGH OF THE UNEMPLOYED . . . 138

MORS JANUA VITÆ 140

TO ALTHEA . . 141

'ΑΠΟΚΑΡΑΔΟΚΙΑ . . 143

LOST AND FOUND 145

THE IDEAL AND THE ACTUAL 147

EPIGRAM . . 148

TO R. W. EMERSON . . 149

SICK-LISTED . . . 150

TO V. F. S. 153

FROM "THE ORDER OF THE BEAN" . . . 155

THE ORDER OF MELCHIZEDEC . . . 156

TO A "BLACK-FELLOW" . . 158

TO TENNYSON 162

A NEW LITTLE WOMAN 164

"AMOR DEI ET PROXIMI" . . . 165

HEINE'S GRAVE 166

RELIGION 167

DIALOGUE. 169

NATURAL LAW IN THE SPIRITUAL WORLD . . 172

SPRING 174

viii　　　　*CONTENTS.*

	PAGE
DE PROFUNDIS	176
DANTE	179
WOMAN'S RIGHTS	180
THE SONG OF THE BILLY	182
EPITHALAMIUM	185
AD VERECUNDIAM	186
FEAR NOT, LITTLE FLOCK	187
JAMESON'S RIDE	188
IN A SWISS CHURCHYARD	190
DAVOS LAKE	196

TO ALTHEA.

TIME was when victors spread their spoils
    From battlefield or racing-post
    Before her feet who pleased them most,
And claimed her blessing on their toils.

I am no victor, spoils have none ;
    But I have woven from my heart
    Some webs of fancy, and my art
Invokes your blessing, dearest one.

A slight, grey-coloured, ragged thing,
    Perchance 'twill sparkle in your sight
    With dewdrops, in the morning light
Of quick-eyed girlhood's sunny spring !

2

TO ALTHEA.

A hovering thought that hurries by
   No common flower, but bee-like seeks
   Its hidden honey, thro' the weeks
That shame the idle butterfly,

Has gathered in a thirsty land
   A little pollen here and there,
   And you, who relish homely fare,
Now hold its measure in your hand.

Perchance some elder may be drawn
   To follow thought but hinted here ;
   And, from a glimmer faintly clear,
To read some promise of the dawn.

I cannot write the thing I see ;
   For who could sweep from midnight skies
   The northern lights, and flash his prize
To dazzle incredulity ?

I can but witness, " I have seen,"
   And bid the crowd of doubters climb
   Where mists no longer dim, nor grime
Of their own chimneys comes between.

Far be it from my hand to draw
   Your lingering footsteps from the wall
   Which you have learnt to love and call
The measure of eternal law.

God's spirit breathed the light and air
   Which fill your garden ; nor will I
   Protest you cannot see the sky
Because I wot it spreads elsewhere.

A tribute-wreath in earlier days,
   The memory of our lost one claimed,
   Whence I have gathered and re-named
Some fading flowerets and sprays ;

And those with these, the scant grain reapt
   Of varying moods in barren years
   That knew no watering but the tears
Of Sisyphean toil, accept !

THE MIGRATION OF THE MUSES.

ARGUMENT.

In the time of Homer, Venus was in low repute among the Greeks. Throughout his books we do not meet with any allusions to her worship. In fact he seems to take every opportunity of "snubbing" her, so to speak. Then, however, Greece flourished. But when Aphrodite became the influential goddess that we subsequently find her, then the woes of Greece began, and when she finally asserted her supremacy, then Greece was reduced to degradation : she was conquered by the Romans, but her conquerors introduced into Rome the proud trophies of her marvellous civilisation, and increased their own splendour by her arts and sciences. But with Grecian culture came Grecian vices, and we view the fall of Rome under circumstances sadly similar to those attendant on the ruin of Greece. Such is, in very digested form, the leading idea of the principal part of the poem. The rest describes in brief the introduction of Literature and Art into England, and the subsequent curious concentration of one branch of them in the " Lake District."

WHEN as a warrior to the fight
Came Hellas forth to win a crown,
She turned her cow'ring foes to flight,
And decked herself with fair renown.

With haughty hand and dauntless heart
She dared the world to do its worst ;
Pallas Invicta took her part,
And led her legions from the first.

Her hardy warriors loved to live
Encamped upon the martial plain ;
'Mid clashing arms their pride to strive,
Despising loss, ignoring pain.

'Twas theirs a soldier's life to spend,
Their canopy the open sky ;
Exulting ! free !—and this their end,
To *dare*, to *conquer*, or to *die*.

But when she laid aside her bow,
And sheathed the gory sword of Greece ;
When victory wreathed her maiden brow,
And lulled her into dreams of peace ;

To other humours then inclined,
Proud Hellas raised her laurelled head,
Predestined by the trio blind [1]
In works of peace to take the lead.

[1] The Fates.

Then Pallas left the knightly field,
Hung in a fane her unstrung bow,
Laid by for aye her burnished shield,
Henceforth to tend the suppliants' vow.

Then thundering Neptune ceased to roar,
And chase the foe on crested waves,
To whisper with the Nymphs on shore,
And woo the Mermaids in the caves.

Then, hushed upon his placid breast,
The ships-of-battle gently swayed ;
Round keels which corpses lately prest
The wanton dolphins idly played.

Then skilled Apollo with his lyre
To teach the bards of Hellas came ;
And gods and goddesses conspire
To lead her on the path to fame.

A lovely spot the Muses chose,
Upon a verdant mountain-top—
Where the sweet stream Cephisus flows,
Where Venus often loved to stop,

THE MIGRATION OF THE MUSES.

To lave her tresses in the streams,
Smile at her image in the pool,
And lose herself in fancy's dreams
Among the rushes' verdure cool.

There, where the weeping willows droop,
And lilies strew the shady bowers,
Fair Aphrodite loved to stoop
And bind her locks with varied flowers.[1]

But Venus was a shameless maid,
Nor honour was among her train ;
And with whatever folk she stayed,
Her presence was a certain bane.

But she was apt-to-please, and fair,
Whole cities yielded to her sway—
Tho' from the day they yielded, there
Commenced their downfall and decay.

[1] τοῦ καλλινάου τ' ἀπὸ Κηφισοῦ ῥοὰς
τὰν Κύπριν κλῄζουσιν ἀφυσσαμέναν
χώραν καταπνεῦσαι μετρίας ἀνέμων
ἡδυπνόους αὔρας· ἀεὶ δ' ἐπιβαλλομέναν
χαίταισιν εὐώδη ῥοδέων πλόκον ἀνθέων
τᾷ σοφίᾳ παρέδρους πέμπειν ἔρωτας,
παντοίας ἀρετᾶς ξυνεργοῦς·—EURIP

But Venus, wandering 'mid the hills,
Spied Hellas at her work beneath,
And, tripping past the trickling rills,
Approached her with a rosy wreath.

Bright as the glancing sunbeams glow
At even, o'er the mountain peaks
She smiled, as if her love to show,
And kissed the maiden's blushing cheeks.

Quoth she, " Sweet maid, tho' lately met,
I as a sister love thee well ;
This of thy favours let me get—
Within thy bulwarks leave to dwell !

" Oft have I watched thee from the height,
And marked thy business in the dale ;
'Neath chaste Diana's favouring light
Strayed with thy subjects thro' the vale.

" O rear for me a comely pile,
Grant me to make with thee my home "—
She paused :—vain Hellas with a smile
The fatal answer rendered—" Come !

THE MIGRATION OF THE MUSES.

" Come, gentle Venus, dwell with me !
Come ! in my cities found thy throne !
Thy willing subjects will we be ;
Come, and claim all things for thine own !

" Goddess, of all to men most kind,
We hail thine advent as a boon ;
A hearty welcome dost thou find,
Come,—for thou canst not come too soon ! "

Thus Hellas spake, and thus declared
How mists of darkness dimmed her eyes ;
For flattery had her mind prepared
To yield herself a willing prize.

Ah ! little dreamt she of the net
She spread around her wily feet,
When Hellas Aphrodite met,
And with her charmer stayed to treat !

O not the first, sweet Hellas, thou,
To yield thyself to Venus' sway !
But where her former clients now ?—
And where—Oh ! where art *thou* to-day ?

Thus Eve, the mother of our race,
Fair words and promises ensnared,
Found speedy ruin, and disgrace
For all her progeny prepared.

So Venus held her court in Greece,
All offices her creatures filled ;
Lust, Luxury, and slothful Ease,
Enforced her edicts as she willed.

Rejected Virtue fled dismayed,
Ejected with a ruthless hand ;
Unkempt, in tattered garment strayed,
A houseless outlaw o'er the land.

The palaces she lately blest
Before her face their portals shut ;
Nor could she, weary, find a rest
Within the lowly shepherd's hut.

But were this lay designed to tell
The sorrows of unhappy Greece,
How step by step from fame she fell,
I know not when my song should cease.

And tho' the Muses' ancient fire
Still burned as in the brighter days,
'Twas Venus tuned the poets' lyre,
And bade them only sing her praise.

When war's shrill clarion again
Bade Greece defend her wasting lands,
She drew her rusty sword in vain,
And fled before the hostile bands.

This then her end ! dishonoured, mean,
She drained her bitter cup of woe ;
And Hellas, who had lived a queen,
Became the bond-slave of a foe.

Then, from their grotto on the hill,
The conquerors take the Muses home,
And found for them, with hearty will,
A mansion on the hills of Rome.

The gods from Mount Olympus came,
Jove granted Zeus co-equal rights ;
They shared the sacrificial flame,
Co-partners in divine delights.

They covenanted and decreed
That Rome should equal honours pay
To Greek and Roman gods ;—agreed
To share their provinces of sway.

Then elocutionary art,
The Lord of Rhetoric, Hermes, taught ;
And for the harp with merry heart
The Romans blithe Apollo sought.

Then flourished Rome, as tho' the sun,
Bursting the clouds, shone brightly clear
And pausing in his course begun,
Prolonged the summer all the year.

Greece lay in ruins ! nothing left
But shattered traces of the past,—
As towering cliffs by tempests reft,
Or oaks by ruthless lightning blast.

But lo ! upon the stones that erst
The bulwark stood of Athens' pride,
Sat she who had her patron curst,—
Sat her misfortune to deride.

Beneath her feet fair Hellas lay :—
Fair Hellas ?—she who *once* was fair,
But now ! mute be the word, nor say
How changed, how sadly changed her air.

But Aphrodite grimly smiles
Upon the ruin she hath wrought ;
On fallen glory's crumbling piles,
And crushes other realms in thought.

Then rising on the wings of night,
She soared to seek another home ;
Robed as a seraph of the light
She paused before the gates of Rome.

Gladly to her the Romans gave
The choicest honours of the gods ;
Rome was her self-delivered slave—
Rome felt the smarting of her rods.

Yes ; fascinated, she endured
The bitter sweetness of her sway,
By dazzling vanities allured,
As serpents charm the trembling prey.

Till Rome like Greece went down, down, down,
The mightier power harder dies ;
For the strong lion will not drown
In pools that drown the struggling flies.

Slowly but surely see her droop—
She struggles—but her foes deride—
The foeman made but one fell swoop,
And scattered to the winds her pride.

She, who had ground beneath her heel
Vast nations, an unconquered queen,
'Twas hers the ruthless sword to feel ;
Her blood must fertilise the green ;

Her children feel the captor's might,
Her coffers fill the captor's store,
Her treasures be her foes' delight,
Herself her foes' for evermore.

The lingering Muses fail to find
A patron in the conqueror rude ;
Barbarians of uncultured mind
Leave them to pine in solitude.

Full soon they leave the mossy cove,
And verdant dells they long had blest ;
And listless o'er the countries rove,
To seek where they may find a rest.

They paused in many a lovely place,
Of them did many a region boast,
Where still their footsteps we may trace—
And reached at last bright Albion's coast.

Here, here they found a glad retreat,
Scattered their blessings far and wide ;
And gaily fixed their central seat
Upon Helvellyn's rugged side.

Skiddaw outstretched his sheltering arm,
Protection lent the gruff Scawfell ;
The Muses found a welcome warm
From mountain, plain, lake, tarn and dell.

The pastoral plains their music lent
To many an ardent poet's lyre ;
Unstintingly was fuel spent
To feed the re-enkindling fire.

Historians sought the shady groves
And grassy slopes of Windermere,
Where, wrapt in meditation, roves
The manifold philosopher !

The water-nymphs their forms survey
In canvas mirrors on the shore ;
And envious art would fain display
The thundering waters of Lodore.

Then—hold ! it is not meet that I,
With halting verse, the theme expand ;
Such scenes as these for artists cry,
To copy with an abler hand.

Here roughly sketched you may behold
The paths of ruin and of fame ;
View Virtue spoilèd of her gold,
And Vice triumphant in her shame.

Here heathen names one may detect,
And heathen imagery trace ;
Yet muddy waters may reflect
The image of a noble face.

And from the realms of darkened thought,
And mazes of mythology,
Some straggling sunbeams may be sought
To sparkle in a brighter sky.

Greece ! where are now thy stately halls ?
Thy mansions towering to the sky ?—
'Mid what were once rich temple walls
Resounds the bittern's mournful cry.

The storm-king roars on mountain-tops,
Does battle with the foaming wave ;
Then, sweeping onward—see ! he stops
To sit and sigh upon thy grave.

Rome ! where art thou ? Thou answerest, " Lo !
Where erst I stood."   But where thy might ?
Gone, as before the sun the snow,
Thou, like one robbed of health's delight.

   *   *   *   *

Then, Britons, be not tamely led,
When Vice would press deceptive suit !
But, 'neath the centaur's human head,
Beware the body of a brute !

FAREWELL.

DEAR little aching heart, farewell !
  Thy patient sufferings o'er,
Henceforth with Christ 'tis thine to dwell,
  And " thou shalt weep no more."

But O ! thy place of thee bereft,
  Can filled be never more ;
To us this consolation left—
  " Not lost, but gone before ! "

THE PRIVY COUNSELLOR.

IT happened, as with interest I glanced
The pages of a lady's album o'er,
Upon a proverb written there I chanced
To let my eye fall, as on many more—
    " Doe ye nexte thinge."

Here where the wonted proverb meets the eye,
And apt quotations speak from every page,
Precept and sentiment together vie—
'Twas here I met my friend the old adage,
    " Do ye nexte thinge."

Yes ; he is old ! more to be prized for that,
Older mayhap than many a rival there ;
But seldom quoted he is never " flat,"
And gives good counsel still to all who hear ;
    " Doe ye nexte thinge."

I mark the difference in the line of thought,
That led the writers to select their themes ;
Some love, some truism, sentiment :—a sort
Of picture gallery of hearts this seems—
　　　　" Doe ye nexte thinge."

Ah ! this injunction, simple tho' it be,
In olden English, nor in flowery verse
Nor foreign garb, as many here I see,
Contains a sermon to the point and terse—
　　　　" Doe ye nexte thinge."

Thanks, trusty counsellor ! thy word shall guide
My doubtful footsteps, when the mists of life
Obscure my vision, and the prospect hide ;
Then strong in faith, fain would I, bating strife,
　　　　" Doe ye nexte thinge."

DISAPPOINTMENT.

THUS, as the blossoms of a promised crop,
Nipped by the frosts of winter loth to part,
Point to fair fruit, but in the pointing drop—
So fail the expectations of my heart !

Or, as when snowflakes carried by the breeze,
Glance for a moment on the thankless plain,
Then melting vanish, while succeeding these
Drop others softly where the first have lain ;

So 'tis with life ! one sinks, another springs
Into the gap ; the stream unchecked |flows by,
And countless lives upon its bosom brings,
Like racing straws with which young children vie :

On, whirling on ; and if one foul or sink,

Its heedless rivals past it hurry on ;

None, but its watcher from the streamlet's brink,

Dismayed perceives his little straw has gone !

A CHILD'S PLAINT.

O EDIE, how I miss thee !
　I miss thee every day,
In every occupation,
　In all my work and play !

Dear sister, can I ever
　Forgetful prove of thee ?
O, not till time shall sever
　The links of memory !

My playmate from the cradle,
　My comrade day by day,
A sharer in my studies,
　A partner in my play.

What care I tho' the roses
　Bloom sweetly on the wall,
Or that the fragrant posies
　Well flourish in the hall ?

For surely they, tho' gaily
    Arrayed in living green,
Look down upon me daily,
    And mourn the roses' queen.

And other hands must water
    The plants that once were thine ;
But who shall pluck the blossoms,
    And proudly call them " mine " ?

Thy garden still is blooming,
    From weeds kept fairly free,
But now to pluck the flowers
    Is plucking thorns for me !

Thy rockery deserted,
    No ferns or flowers grace ;
None yet so callous-hearted
    To move it from its place.

O where the busy fingers
    That bettered all around,
That scattered seeds of kindness
    On every open ground ?

O where thy buoyant laughter,
   The eyes that brimmed with fun,
The limbs that loved to scramble,
   The feet that loved to run?

O where—but stop, the query
   Re-echoes from the wall,
And never will my sister
   Respond with cheery call.

In every thing around me
   I find reflected thee;
And every common object
   Strikes chords of memory.

Thy corner of the table,
   Thy seat at morning prayer,
Are vacant—but they speak of
   The time when thou wast there!

The path we travelled daily
   To lessons, you and I,
I now alone must traverse—
   Alone—alone—for aye!

The old familiar lessons,
  (Tho' never loved, you know)
Since I've not thee to share them,
  Are far, far harder now.

And tho' I win my prizes,
  Whom shall I show my toy,
And have its value doubled
  By having shared the joy ?

Thy seat in church is empty,
  And gaps are all around,
But O ! by far the deepest
  Within my heart is found.

I love to trace thy fingers,
  E'en where they made a stain ;
And mischief wrought by thee, dear,
  Strange value seems to gain.

The hymns by thee beloved,
  The texts that thou didst write,
For me have gained a lustre,
  Like gems made triply bright.

The plant that climbs the trellis
  Around the entrance way,
Will ne'er to thee, its planter,
  Thy careful skill repay.

In size and shade and verdure
  Increasing more and more,
All eyes but thine it pleaseth
  When entering by the door.

But O ! I am so lonely ;
  I'll never, never be
Accustomed to thine absence,
  My own dear darling E——.

And tho' thou ne'er returnest,
  I cannot call thee dead ;
I feel as tho' a journey
  Were keeping thee instead.

But no ! thy journey's over—
  Lone journeying waits for me ;
And thou art lying sleeping
  Beyond the deep blue sea !

Still tho' I'm very lonely,
 I will not fret or cry,
For I shall meet my Edie
 In heaven by and by.

I must be up and active,
 And have a cheerful face,
For I must both be Allie,
 And try take Edie's place.

Soon waiting will be over,
 And then again we'll meet,
A family united,
 Around the mercy-seat.

Then shall we know the reason
 Why Edie went before ;
And I shall find my darling,
 And never lose her more.

THE SALE OF THE FRENCH CROWN JEWELS.

Relics of a Regal sway !
Relics of a better day !
Relics of a country blest
In the bygone years with rest !
Sad memorial of a time
Fraught with every kind of crime :
Murder, plunder, dire distress,
Money matters in a " mess " ;
Bankruptcy and discord rife,
Thousands yielding guiltless life ;
Strife within and strife without,
Cannons' roar and victors' shout ;
Till Napoleon, in command,
Kept in check with giant hand
Anarchy, and turned his arms

In pursuit of foreign palms ;
Ground beneath his iron sway,
Countries yielding to dismay,
Till he was himself checkmated
When at Waterloo defeated !

All that speaks of better days
Will France sell to him who pays ?

FOR A CHRISTMAS CARD.

"PEACE on the earth,"
With holy mirth,
The heavenly anthem raise ;
Let earth rejoice
And lend her voice
The Saviour king to praise ;
And be the chorus loud as then,
When angels sang—"Goodwill to men."

TRANSLATION.

HORACE.

WHILE none other lived by thee
More beloved, whose arms might be
Thrown around thy neck so white,
Passing kings' was my delight !

LYDIA.

While within thine ardent breast
Was no room for greater guest,
Chloë after Lydia came,
Mine was then as Ilia's fame.

HORACE.

Thracian Chloë now me sways,
Skilled in dances, well she plays ;
For her I would gladly give
Even life, if she might live.

LYDIA.

Calaïs now with mutual fires,
Son of Ornythus, me inspires,
For whom life I *twice* would give,
Would fate suffer him to live.

HORACE.

What if Venus, passed away,
Bring us back beneath her sway?
Chloë driven from the door,
Lydia be received once more?

LYDIA.

Be he brighter than a star,
Thou more wild than Hadria,
Lighter than a cork, yet I
Glad with thee will live and die!

THE FIRST LOVE-SONG.

Come into the garden, Eve,
    Bone of my very bone ;
Joy doth my swelling heart upheave,
    No longer now alone.

Better than all my ribs,
    In this sequester'd nook,
Clad in our fig-leaf bibs
    We'll feast,—and you'll be cook.

Happy together thus
    We'll pass a joyful life ;
Thou bearing all the fuss
    And making none, my wife !

A JUBILEE SONG.

Air : "*Austria.*"

Sound it loud throughout the kingdom
  Which we boast of as our home,
Let the breezes sweep it swiftly
  O'er the boundless ocean's foam,
To the countries of the tropics,
  To the islands of the north ;
Yea, throughout the realm she governs
  Let the joyful sound go forth—
      'Tis Victoria's Jubilee !

Let the country where the Ganges
  Pours its sacred floods along,
Join with hearty voice in singing
  This our glad triumphant song ;

Let the newly-added Burmah
    With her conquerors compete,
For her victors brought her freedom,
    So to hail their Queen 'tis meet,—
        'Tis Victoria's Jubilee !

Let the lands the Queen has governed
    Now for fifty years rejoice ;
Let New Zealand and Australia
    With Tasmania lend their voice ;
Let the isles off Afric's coastline,
    With the Southern isles as well,
Canada and Cape conspire
    This our gladsome song to swell—
        'Tis Victoria's Jubilee !

Let the creeds of every nation
    That beneath her sceptre bend,
With a joyful mind, and hearty,
    Their resounding voices lend.
Let the nations look in wonder
    At the joy which we display ;
Tell them, as they stand and marvel,
    Why our Fatherland's so gay—
        'Tis Victoria's Jubilee !

'Tis not she whom nature worships,
  'Tis not she whom we proclaim,
'Tis the God who in His mercy
  Made her symbol of our fame ;
Who for fifty years hath given
  Peace with honour, under one
Whom He made the Queen of regions
  Whereon never sets the sun—
          'Tis Victoria's Jubilee !

EPITAPH.

Here lieth one, tho' not long dead,
Was twenty years confined to bed ;
And all that time, O dire disgrace,
Was said to never wash her face !

IN MEMORIAM.

A. L. M.

A FRIEND, a counsellor, a trusty guide
Of youthful tourists on the mountain track,
Leading to knowledge ; well we might confide
To him the interests that we ne'er held back.

Genial, kindhearted, by his equals loved,
Respected by his juniors, with respect
Not born of mere formality, but moved
By admiration of his intellect.

A mind that, lightning-like, o'er storm-clouds dark,
Flash'd on its path of light from pole to pole
Yet stooped to kindle up the glimmering spark
To light the candle of a lesser soul.

His spirit hath returned to God who gave,
Called higher in his half-completed race ;
Re-entering through the portals of the grave—
We're thankful he was granted us a space !

He rests ! he rests ! his knowledge is complete ;
Still up the steep our labouring footsteps tend ;
One lacks a guardian to direct his feet ;
One, guide ; one, teacher ; aye, and ALL a FRIEND.

DEATH.

"We understand death for the first time when he puts his hands upon one whom we love."—*Madame de Staël.*

No ! Death, we cannot *understand* thee so !
'Tis then we know thy power, feel thy might,
When thou dost all our towers of hope o'erthrow,
And turn our noonday into blackest night.

O Death ! when thou dost wrench from bleeding
    hearts
The tendrils that have clung to them so long,
Giving and taking strength which each imparts—
Ah ! then we realise that thou art strong.

But still we do not *understand* thee ; while
We tremble at thy presence, we confess
We scarce know why we shudder, or recoil
To touch a body that is spiritless.

Who art thou, Death, and wherefore come and
    whence ?
Science is speechless—can we nothing say
Of all the dear ones thou dost hurry hence ?—
" In Heaven's keeping we are safe, and they."

.

YOU AND I.

" JENNY, being New Year's Day,
                              You and I
Well may rest a-while, and stay
                              Peacefully ;
Take a holiday for both,
You, I'm sure, are nothing loth,
                              Nor am I.

We have trudged along together,
                              You and I ;
We have braved life's stormy weather,
                              You and I ;
Yes, for many and many a day
We have tramped our chequered way,
                              You and I.

YOU AND I.

Tho' the way was often rough,
     You and I
Were composed of sterner stuff
     Than to cry ;
But when hardships thrown among,
We just fought our way along,
     You and I.

When the tempest bellowed loud,
     You and I
Saw the light behind the cloud
     Constantly ;
Ah ! it soon came bursting thro',
And delightful days we knew,
     You and I.

Yes, the sun shone brightly clear
     Up on high,
And we'd nothing left to fear,
     You and I ;
So we blithely tripped along,
Like the music of a song,
     You and I.

But the clouds grew thick again
                Frequently,
And sent down the pelting rain
                From the sky ;
Overhead the thunder clashed,
In our eyes the lightning flashed,
                Fearfully.

But we did not sit and mope,
                You and I ;
No, we trudged along in hope,
                Patiently ;
'Till we saw the sun again,
Gleaming brightly thro' the rain,
                You and I.

Folk were often good and kind,
                Frequently ;
Often cruel, *we* didn't mind,
                You and I ;
But we held on gaily yet,
Whatsoever sort we met,
                You and I.

Jenny, many a day has fled
                              Quickly by,
But we've never lacked for bread,
                              You and I.
We are older than we were,
But we still may do and dare,
                              You and I.

Tho' a mingled lot we've seen,
                              You and I,
This our watchword true has been,
                              ' Ne'er say die';
So we little recked what came,
And we've won our share of fame,
                              You and I.

We have saved a little sum,
                              You and I,
Lest a rainy day should come,
                              By and by ;
We should grateful be, my pet,
We've no need to use it yet,
                              You and I.

With our path before us clear
            You and I
Thus commence another year
            Hopefully ;
We will hold along our way,
Living on from day to day,
            You and I.

So we'll never mind the weather,
            You and I,
But we'll pull along together
            Cheerfully,
Sure while we're both united,
At nought we need be frighted,
            You and I.

Then we'll let the rain come down
            Till it soak,
And we'll trudge along the town
            In a cloak ;
We'll never lack nor hunger."
Thus spake the costermonger
            To his " moke."

A PLAY ON THE LAST MINSTREL.

THE time was long, the room was cold,
The Lecturer was infirm and old ;
His bristling cheek, and ragged hair,
Proved he had little time to spare
From the perusal of his books
To add improvement to his looks.
His notes, his sole remaining joy,
Were made when Merlin was a boy.
The first of all professors he,
Of logical anatomy ;
And, well-a-day ! his compeers said,
What *should* we do if he were dead ?
No more on prancing hunter borne,
He revelled in the echoing horn ;

No longer jovially as once,

High placed in hall, he swiped the sconce,

Or at the "Smoker" blithely sang

The deeds of Pyramus O'Bang ;

No longer, on the water's edge,

He coursed the rats among the sedge.

Old times were changed, old manners gone,

A stranger filled the Vice's throne :

The Proctors of that iron time

Had called this harmless art a crime !

No more, by strenuous use of "crams,"

He came out well in all exams.

A toiling Fellow, proudly poor,

He sat behind his double door,

And hammered into brains amazed

The lore examiners had praised.

He lived hard by, where old Tom Tower

Looks out upon the River Lower,

And proudly sloped about the town

Bedizened in an M.A. gown.

At length approached his dallying fame,

He an Examiner became,

And with determined step at last

The em*battle*d portal arch he passed,

5

Whose massy bar and poderous grate
Had oft repulsed the candidate;
And oft had closed the panels wide
Against an onset three times tried.
The Clerk had marked the weary pace,
The time-worn warrior's long-drawn face,
And on his *page* would sadly tell
The shillings he had lost as well!
Ah! well he knew adversity
Attended on a " *high degree;* "
And fallen pride had shed her tear
On the Testamur's frequent bier.

When fees our hero's purse supplied,
Then, with his pocket, grew his pride;
And he began to talk anon
Of shining as a greater don!
Fain a professor would he be,
So ran the signal up—" D.D."
A braver ne'er essayed the post,
He was the noblest of the host
Of those who tried to split the hairs
Of præ-historical affairs.
His pen would many a tale employ

Of the old warriors of Troy ;
And he could cite each point where *B*
With codex *A* did disagree.
No problem could his soul perplex,
For should it try, he called it " X " ;
And sooner than it takes to write,
'Twas all as clear as black and white.
The humble boon was soon obtained ;
The new Professor audience gained.
But, when he reached the lecture hall,
Where were his hearers mustered all,
Perchance they wished his boon denied,
For when he exegesis tried,
His trembling voice had lost the ease
Which marks security to please ;
And undergraduates strove in vain
To catch the dribblings of his brain ;
And waited, yawning, till the chime
Should tell the close of lecture time.
And then said he, full fain he would
They'd hearken to his *notes* so good.
For undergrads they were not framed,
But for high scholars widely famed :
He'd printed extracts in reviews,

And other literary news.

Among the *notes* his fingers strayed,

And an unwise selection made !

And oft he shook his hoary head,

And quoth, " We'll take this one instead."

But when he came to μὲν and δέ

The old man raised his face with glee,

And lighted up his faded eye

With all a scholar's ecstasy.

With varying cadence, soft or strong,

He told the graces that belong,

The power latent, nobly grand,

" On this " and " on the other hand."

The present scene, the future lot,

His " hums " and " haws " were all forgot ;

His stammering tongue, and age's frost

In the full tide of speech were lost.

" Each blank in human works," said he,

" Is well supplied with μὲν and δέ ;

If any passage be abstruse,

You'll easily solve it by their use ;

MEN by itself is useless quite,

But add a ΔE, and all is right.

Like Eve, Δέ is a good helpmeet

To aid the *men*, else incomplete ;
What if for long you've sought in vain
The drift of some stiff clause to gain !
Try this,—you'll conquer in the end,
For " it is never too late to μεν-δε."

PULPIT RHETORIC.

He preached not Christ ;
He preached with eloquence, and knew it well ;
He preached *of* Christ,
But tried to hold us with the magic spell
Of his own oratory :
                          With a useless skill
Touched up the picture he presented, till
Its sweet sublimity was nigh concealed.
Would he had left the paint and brush alone,
Drawn back the curtain o'er the portrait thrown,
The speaking picture self-complete revealed !

TO D. M. J.

Thou that art brightest,
Dearest and lightest,
Skipping so softly o'er life's rugged way ;
Fearing no sorrow,
Dreading no morrow,
Joyfully grasping the joys of to-day ;

Thou, like a butterfly,
Gaily dost flutter by
Brambles and thistles that grow by the way ;
Eagerly sighting,
Daintily lighting
On every floweret smiling and gay.

Gladly they wait for thee,
Decked out in state for thee,
Nodding a welcome, they bid thee approach ;

Blushing in varied charms,
Waving their leafy arms—
"Come, little wanderer, come and encroach."

Lightly the Zephyrs play—
Dance with the flowerets gay—
Dance to the music which breathes thro' the trees;
Hush ! whispering !—down the lane,
See ! they whirl off again,
Bow to their partners, and flit on the breeze.

Come, little maiden gay,
Gather them while you may,
Gather the flowers that bloom at your feet ;
Day is but dawning yet—
Who can tell, little pet,
Who knows what later wayfarers you'll meet ?

See, they are smiling,
Nodding, beguiling,
Bidding thee pluck them and wear next thy heart ;
Flowers may soon be past,
Briars may spring up fast,
Thorns on thy pathway before thee may start.

Pluck them ;—but even so
Soon they will fade, I know,
Yet you'll remember that once they were sweet ;
Flowers that never die
You'll gather by and by,
Flowers that angels shall heap at your feet !

But as you upward move,
Think of this, little love,
Flowers will often be found upon weeds ;
Don't pass them idly by,
Gather them tenderly,
But, dear, be careful—don't scatter the seeds.

Sow, as you upward move,
Sow little seeds of love,
Plant little plantlets for others to find ;
Sowing for others,
Sisters and brothers,
Double you'll learn is the joy of the kind !

ORTHOGRAPHY.

THE worldling views his shattered hopes
    Fall crumbling to the ground,
Writes "disappointment" on the heap,
    And in the waves is drown'd.
The Christian sees the angry floods
    His darling schemes immerge,
Sighs " His appointment !" and refreshed,
    Arises from the surge.

MAGDALEN FANCIES.

In the chill hour of early dawn,
When night her mantle had withdrawn
But scarcely from the sleeping town,
I stood on Magdalen's hoary crown.

The morning mists enveloped still
The little ridge of distant hill;
But as I gazed they rolled away
Before the sun's returning sway.

The city, slumbering at my feet,
Arose returning day to greet,
Fresh from the haziness of night,
Appeared to blink before the light.

Ere Orient portals opening wide,
Emit Aurora's gorgeous pride,
The morning star had sunk to rest
Upon the bosom of the West.

Now signs of life salute mine eyes,
And sounds of movement upward rise ;
And the calm, peaceful dream of morn
Is broken by the May-Day horn.

Hark !—one ! two ! three ! four ! five !—the hour,
Tolled from the venerable tower,
Recalls me from my reverie
To undefined expectancy.

Then, as the last stroke's quivering tones
Are whispered by the embattled stones
To the hushed Zephyrs passing by,
Ascends an anthem to the sky.

Boy-voices raise a glad refrain,
The passing breezes catch the strain,
And bear the sweet, expiring breath
To the expectant crowd beneath.

They cease ! but on the stillness swells
The grander music of the bells :
From side to side the belfry rocks
Beneath the thrice-repeated shocks.

Silence again ; all's over now,
And I descend once more below ;
Into the prosy paths of life,
Into the world's reopening strife.

But, Magdalen, can I ever be
Forgetful of this hour on thee ;
Blest from thy summit to survey
The waking of the " First of May !"

AN AMERICAN TRAGEDY IN A NUT-SHELL.

A BOAT, a sailor, the sea ;

A gust, a billow,—where's he ?

A corpse, a lantern, the lea ;

A parting, a weeping,—a she ;

A coroner—" Fell o' de sea."

"SIGNÔRA WRANGLER."

I.

Miv.

MAN, on his pinnacle of pride,
Indulged in Fancy's sweetest dream ;
There sat no woman by his side
Who might dispute his sway supreme.

He watched them climbing—saw them stop
Half-way—while still he held the lead ;
But *thou* hast scaled the veriest top,
And snatched the laurels from his head !

Lady, well done ! 'tis not the last
Or fairest triumph of your brain ;
But oh ! beware ye do not cast
Too much aside such spoils to gain !

For what are learning, old and new,
And lists of honours nobly won,
Unless the heart be light and true ?—
We warn, as we repeat "WELL DONE!"

II.

Δἑ.

O Amazonian female thou !
You *beat* the senior wrangler !—how ?
Pray was it with the "wooden spoon"
You mashed the poor unlucky coon ?
Say, who the quarrelling began,
And what annoyed you in the man ?
Women were wranglers since the Fall,
But *thou* art champion of them all !

THE SEA-GULL.

Happy and careless, blythe and free,
Skimming along on the rolling sea,
Riding secure on the crested wave,
Bird of the foam, what a life you have !

Diving below for your finny prey,
Snatching it up—then away, away,
Off to the home in the fortress-rock,
Nestled secure from the tempest shock.

Wandering over the main by night,
Screeching and fluttering round the light,
High on the beacon's quivering mast,
Whence are the signals of danger cast.

6

Hovering low where the hurricane lowers,
Scorning the storm-king's terrible powers,
Floating on foam-topped mountain seas,
Breasting the gale to the cliffs with ease.

Gathering food on the wrinkled sand,
Whirling aloft o'er the sun-dried strand,
Now on the billow again,—and now
Dashing ashore on thy wings of snow!

Rollicking child of the ocean, say
Whether is this thy work or play?
Hast thou ever a pang of care
Spinning about in the limpid air?

Bird of the ocean, wild and free,
Hast thou a little word for me?
Aye, 'tis this—Whatever the sky,
Ever go forward—never say " Die ! "

MYSTERIES OF GRACE.

ALMIGHTY Father, shall I seek
　To quibble at Thy will ?
No ! make me faithful, silent, meek,
　To wonder and be still.

Some awful secret underlies
　Thy dealings with mankind ;
A mystery that, unsolved, defies
　Our straining powers of mind.

But ever clearer grows the light
　As upward still we move ;
Till " fear " dissolves within the bright
　Refulgency of " love."

SONNET.

YOUTH, in life's poppy-gardens walks in dreams,
Bright airy fancies of abstracted bliss,
Visions of joy it would not wake to miss;
While vacancy with speculation teems.
Before the curtained future stands "It seems,"
Forecasting possibilities behind;
Uprearing spectre-castles, which the wind
Serves as foundation, till the gilded beams
Fall with a silent crash, swept by the fold
Of the uplifting curtain; now displayed
Range life's realities, pale, stark, and cold;
And youth, awakening, starts aghast, dismayed.
Yet, face to face with Truth, how hard it seems
To look on such fair wrecks and call them dreams!

ICHABOD.

Poor droning mortal !—dare I call you man ?—
  I scarce know whether laughter or compassion
You mostly merit ; and I hardly can
  Dream you are serious, writing in such fashion.

Yet here's your poem—clear in black and white :
  And is *that* your philosophy of life ?
Such yawning drivel, since it sees the light,
  Is worthy less the critic than the knife.

So Nature furnished you with no ideal
  Above the colouring of a meerschaum pipe !
Of life's realities is none so real
  As listless dozing on perpetual "swipe" !

And this while fellow-mortal's cries are sounding
    For every effort every hand can give,—
You think your energy almost astounding
    Because you even " take the fag " to live !

Considering the uninteresting confusion
    Of such a soulless mass of human delft,
I scarcely marvel at your naïve allusion
    To feeling little interest in yourself !

You'd " be an oyster " ! well, I wish you might be :
    Thus your disease at least might breed a pearl ;
Earth has no room for idlers and would lightly
    Watch the wild billows o'er your slumbers swirl.

You think it is a pity you were born ?
    Bah ! so do I, and all the British nation ;
And may that life whose privileges you scorn
    Haste on your glorious prize—" Annihilation."

CHRISTMAS.

MOTHER, listen ! far away
   Throb the sounds of Christmas bells ;
Joy to many a heart to-day
   From the tower his message tells !

Homes are bright with homely joys ;
   Friends long sundered meet once more ;
Reunited girls and boys
   Enter the paternal door.

And my homing spirit flits
   Through the mazes of the past,
To alight where memory sits,
   Faded garlands round her cast.

'Tis the time I love to rove
   'Mid the tombstones of dead years,

Wondering, as I pensive move,
    I can read and shed no tears !

Life gives little heed to death ;
    Life gives little space for woe ;
Just to twine a hasty wreath,
    Cast it on a grave—and go !

Sorrows, strengthened by belief
    That veiled angels ye are sent,
I am happier for my grief,
    Rising peacefully content.

Mother, listen ! clearer now,
    Nearer clash the Christmas bells ;
Joy to many a heart to-day,
    Joy to *us* his message tells !

CHRISTMAS EVE.

THINKING, thinking, thinking,
   In a cosy little room ;
With the sleepy fire blinking
   Thro' the spectre-shadowed gloom.

Dozing, dozing, dozing,
   Dimly conscious—being where ?
Christmas Eve, and I reposing
   In a loving old armchair.

Dreaming, dreaming, dreaming
   Of the days that used to be ;
And departed faces gleaming
   Thro' the chinks of memory.

Waking, waking, waking
    To the thunder of the blast,
And this motto, Fancy's making,
    " To the Future !—Quit the Past !

TO THE SWALLOWS.

On the roof-slating,
Patiently waiting,
Six little swallows at spring of the day ;
Two chirps, and another—
Look ! there's the " mother,"
A flashing of winglets and all are away !

Each with a bright gleam
Glints like a sunbeam,
Scatters the light from his silk-feathered vest ;
Sails round the chimney-stack,
Whirls to the clouds and back,
Proud to have passed from the bonds of the
    nest !

Soon you'll be flying off,
Or you'd be dying off,
Should you delay till the cold winter wind ;
But you are training now
For your long flight, and know
When you must leave by some hint in your
     mind !

Thus it is everything
Earthly and perishing
Finds to the future its present referr'd ;
Learning to chirp and fly
Only in time to die,—
Only in time to migrate like a bird !

There you go ! dash away !
Chirrup and flash away,
Tho' every chirp brings us nearer the end ;
Play-fields of brighter sky
You'll sweep through by and by,
'Till once again you shall hitherward tend !

Well, my love be with you !

Over the sea with you !

Visiting climes I know only in dreams ;

And may such pleasure flow

To all, where'er you go,

As shall move me when I hear your next
  screams !

TO ALTHEA : A WELCOME.

THE dear little den you've deserted so long
 Rejoices to have you again ;
So do I, as I'd tell, had I time, in a song ;
 But I haven't, and therefore refrain :
So just one wee message before you arrive,
 Hurrah ! for a happy return !
Must hurry, because you are nearing the " drive."
 Take this paper kiss, and then burn.

TO H. J.: A CHRISTMAS GREETING.

As clouds distil in falling rain
But to return in rising dew;
So 'tis but yours come back again
When I bestow a gift on you.

They can no better ; nor can I ;
All things return to whence they fall,
Till in the mystic by and by
We rise to God who giveth all !

This book, a symbol, not a prize,
Accept and use or toss on shelf,
Until I may, should Fortune rise,
Attain to give a gift myself !

ARMA VIRUMQUE CANO!

Avaunt, Black Pride, too vilely base,
That lovest listlessly to trace
A lengthy pedigree, and stand
In bloated sloth on claims of race!

Down with that low-souled thought, that can
Place God-sent heroes under ban
As sons of sires of horny hand,
Nor owns the brother in the man!

That base life-blasting taste which would
Prefer to honest hardihood
And unpretentious manliness
A Bar-sinister claim to Blood!

But those who trace unsullied name
Thro' bygone centuries of fame
Their ancestors arightly bless,
Nor can their pride be worthy blame !

But that is ripe for blame which takes
Unearned distinctions' mask, and makes
Its bland and specious features hide
A face that pitying scorn awakes.

And though my crest shall never speak
The title of a visor'd cheek
My shield no arrows glint aside,
Therefrom the memories I'll not break !

These olden signs may be revealed
On many a hard-fought battle-field,
When 'mid the din of arms and men
My sword shall clash upon my shield.

For battles there are yet to fight;
The war of wrong against the right
Is waxing keener now than then
When my name's founder saw the light !

Then forward on a nobler quest
'Than that whereon our ancient crest
Moved in firm phalanx out of camp
At beckoning Duty's first behest !

So shall my scutcheoned Fleurs de lys
Maintain their symbol'd purity ;
My Royal Lion proudly ramp
O'er broken ranks of villainy !

.

A POSTSCRIPT.

SUGARED with many a sentiment sweet,
Scattered at least over more than one sheet,
Filled to the edges, signed and complete;
    A letter is coming for me !

Sealed and addressed, on the chimney-piece laid,
Majesty's phiz in the corner displayed,
Waiting the hand of man, master, or maid.
    A letter is coming for me !

Gripped with a fist-full of others at last,
Some one is taking it somewhither fast,
Into the post office letter-box cast;
    A letter is coming for me !

Pitched on the counter-board flat on its back,
Dated officially—terrible whack !
Tossed with the multitude into a sack;
          A letter is coming for me !

In a cart bumped along many a mile—
Whisked in a sorting-room under a pile,
Soon to proceed by a different style—
          A letter is coming for me !

Whirled in a railway-truck, tearing through space,
Minutes and miles in a neck-to-neck race—
Flopped on a platform with scantiest grace;
          A letter is coming for me !

Swung by a crane creaking under its toil—
[Bah ! what a—powerful perfume—of oil !]
Dumped in a steamer-hold full of such spoil—
          A letter is coming for me !

Fancy depicts it not crossing the sea !
That is too much for my fancy and me—
Soon it is lying once more on the quay;
          A letter is coming for me !

Miles more of shaking and churning and jar,
Jolted on joggily ever so far;
Firmer than mine your insides, letters, are !
  A letter is coming for me !

" Changez pour everywhere, here, si vous plait."
Out again, in again—bang and away!
" Φευ je ne puis pas dicere—mais."
  A letter is coming for me !

What is that tinkling borne to my ear,
Louder and louder, clear and more clear ?
Yes, 'tis the diligence bells that I hear ;
  A letter is coming for me !

Wait : a few minutes' suspense, one or two ;
Eyes on the door-handle—(what else to do ?)—
Enter a servant-maid, " Monsieur, pour vous."
  A letter has come for me !

THE DEATH OF THE DUKE OF CLARENCE
AND AVONDALE.

THERE are times when silence speaks
With more eloquence than words ;
Sympathy magnetic thrills
Through the heart's o'er-straining chords.
Silence is the term of woe ;
Can we utter this our grief ?
Is it not in silent tears
That the mourner finds relief ?

Yet a nation while it strews
Round a tomb the bridal flowers,
Can but murmur faltering words,
Conscious of their feeble powers.

She who lately ruled a heart
That should gain an empire's love,
Not *alone* beside the grave
Weeps a consort's sad remove.
Hurrying time will spread his veil
All too shortly o'er the scene ;
But the veil shall hide the grief
Of a nation with its Queen !

SPERO MELIORA.

Shall I send it ? shall I send it ?
　　Or destroy it ere it go ?
Once despatched I cannot mend it ;
　　Answer, Shall I send it ?—No !

Shall I stop it, shall I stop it,
　　Ere my sorrows I confess ?
Shall I in the post-box drop it ?
　　Answer, Shall I send it ?—Yes !

Yes, I'll send it ; no, I'll keep it ;
　　It can't go : yet, go it must :
One more night I'll oversleep it
　　And to morning judgment trust.

I'm afraid lest by this letter
    I should make her sad again ;
Yet, if I should write much better
    It might give but double pain.

Sad, perhaps, to know my sadness,
    Which, she says, she cannot heal ;
Sadder, thinking nought but gladness,
    And forgetfulness I feel !

If I only knew the motions
    Of her mind, perchance, I might
Glean a few faint scattered notions
    Of the way I ought to write.

If I knew that she would gladly
    Think me happy, careless, then—
Then I'd try, however sadly,
    To seem cheerful by my pen.

But I half believe the chances
    Are she'd really like to know
What my *thoughts* are, not the fancies
    Which from *any* head might flow.

So I fear that I should grieve her
    By my silence or my speech;
And I fainly would relieve her
    Of the trouble due to each.

She's so young, and I've upset her
    Far too much by what I've said;
And I feel this luckless letter
    Must not go, but burn instead.

Yet she'll think, if I write gaily,
    I've forgotten; can she know
Of the dreams that haunt me daily—
    And why should she ?—better so ?

Wait till she's a little older,
    School-work now should fill her mind;
What I have already told her
    Peradventure was unkind.

Yet, I hoped it would be giving,
    For herself as well as me,
Some clear plans for present living
    Training for futurity.

That we'd take a mutual pleasure
  In each other's every state—
Reading, working, times of leisure,
  In the years we had to wait.

Drawing to each other nearer
  As our common interests grew ;
Growing to each other dearer
  As the season closer drew.

I could see that she was laying
  Other plans than mine ahead :
How could I refrain from saying
  That she must take mine instead ?

But she only answered slightly,
  For her heart was full of home ;
And I felt that it was rightly
  That her thoughts refused to roam.

Let her love her home ! I would not
  Lure her from that sacred shrine ;
But I don't see why she could not
  To its other names add mine !

Till the time came to forsake it,
    And to make a home with me,
Surely I would have her make it
    Centre of life's energy.

And if, at the stated season,
    Duty keep her overlate,
What could be sufficient reason
    Why I should not longer wait ?

Now, mayhap, the thoughts are banished
    From her mind, and wisely so ;
But my patient hopes unvanished
    Boldly to the future go :

And I'm thinking, while combining
    Shredded memory's patch-work scraps,
Thinking of a light that's shining
    On " the better side of P'R'APS."

TO MY DOG.

No reason ?   Whence and what is that which I
Cannot express by any other term
Innate within thee ?   " *Instinct* " fails to give
Full comprehension to the multiplex
And many-sided motions of thy brain.

Why should that which in a *child* were reason,
Though mere faint glimmerings of an embryo mind,
In thee, a *dog*, be labelled something less ?
Not that its *signs* are less, mayhap far more,
But *à priori*, since thou art a dog.

Could it dishonour God that we should grant
That lower creatures may possess with man
Far more in common than our fathers thought ?

Nay; rather, 'twere dishonour to deny
To those who hold the substance those same terms
That may express the self-same gifts in both,
The difference rather of degree than kind,
And man is *raised*, not lowered ; for the higher
We shall upraise the lower, still more highly
Shall we exalt the higher ; truth is truth,
But hidden, it is only *darkened* truth,
Yet truth the same, and works unrecognised,
The loser for his blindness, only man.

No soul ?   Instinctively I answer, " No ! "
Yet what is that—some inarticulate
Sympathetic sense—that seems in thee
To hold communion with my unseen self ?
What is that common element that gives
Such mutual understanding resting-place ?
'Tis *there*, I know, but what it *is* know not.

None can as yet define the soul, nor fix
The limits or the intervals that bound
Intercommunications of the mind ;
Or what *is* mind ; or where the mind and soul
Diverge ; what reason is, or limited

To whom, by what ; how sympathy's expressed ;
What *life* implies, or magnetism means ;
Or what the confines of the natural.
So much unknown ; and yet, my dog, I feel
(Feeling may be but knowledge learnt untaught)
There is a deeper, higher part of me
Wherewith thou hast no power to sympathise,
No capability to harmonise,
No faculty for even guessing at,
And no innate criteria to gauge :
Albeit, were I sad in brooding o'er
The trackless vastness of the dark unknown,
Eternal transcendental mysteries
Whose shadowy outlines catch our eyeless sight,
Thou mightest lie by pensively and seem
As sharing just those dreams that weigh me down,
Yet wert thou saddened, 'twould be but because
I was so too, not feeling in thyself
A common interest in a common grief.

Nor would the joy that sometimes stirs my soul
In dwelling on the wondrous works of God
Stir up in thee a joy beyond that felt
In feeling I was happy ; yet at times

Thy yearning, wistful eyes turned up to mine,
Seeming to plead with silent questioning
For explanations that I cannot give,
Draw me the nearer while I feel most far.

For is't not thus we turn our questioning
And yearning glances heavenward to Him
Who knoweth all; while we know nought but that
He hath already taught us; know He loves,
And trust Him for His knowledge and His love?
Oh, fools and blind ! 'tis not despising us
Or in the lofty scorn of majesty
Heedlessly inattentive to our plea,
He grants not satisfaction instantly.

Should I attempt in simplest chosen words
To teach my dog the solar-system's laws,
The changing phases of the moon he bays
Or unseen causes 'neath phenomena,
Those pleading eyes would never brighten up
With apprehensive intellectual light,
Showing some long-worked problem solved at last.

Knowing I cannot thus explain, I lay
My hand upon his shaggy head, and stroke

And pat him lovingly, and say, "Good dog!"
He, bounding off in happy confidence,
Content to know how much he cannot know
And trusting in his master's character.

Thus God with us, while as our finite sense
Is still incapable to bear the whole,
The fullest revelation of Himself
And of eternal verities : Him we trust,
To whom all contradictions, reconciled,
Form one harmonious whole, which He will teach
As we to bear are able.   Oh, forgive,
Great God, the cavillings of our ignorance,
And fit us daily more and more to learn
The lessons that Thy providence would teach ;
Till through imperfect to more perfect grown
We may at last to full perfection come.

8

ON A SWALLOW'S NEST IN THE DOORWAY OF A VILLAGE SCHOOL.

Scorn not to learn although, perchance,
　　The teacher be not great or wise ;
The seeming meanness may enhance
　　The lesson's value in our eyes.

The builder of some glorious pile,
　　That rears aloft its shimmering cone,
Must use the gimlet and the file
　　As well as monster quarried stone.

Nor does our God disdain to take
　　For instruments the " weak " and " small,"
By them Himself to work, and make
　　His message echo through them all.

There's not a flower too small to add
  Its answer to the stars above,
To cheer some heart, forlorn and sad,
  Who trembling questions, " Is God Love ? "

And, little swallow, who didst set
  Thy wattled hut amid these beams,
From thee a lesson we may get—
  A lesson greater than it seems.

Of quietness and confidence,
  And daily duties daily done,
Instinctive trust transcending sense,
  Of steady purpose, dreading none.

Such lessons learning we shall give
  Our thanks to thee for building here ;
And acting on them daily live
  More nobly till you come next year !

   *   *   *   *

O foolish impulse, false to thought !
  " Instinctive trust ! "—an idle phrase !
A reasoned doubt, tho' dearly bought,
  Were worthier of a reasoned praise.

O swallow, blindly led by sense
 Of outward things thro' wonted skies;
And yearly hurried here and hence
 By carnal need of sun and flies !

False is the fancy that would find
 Faith's symbol in a sinless hen ;
Far nobler to the thoughtful mind
 Is man with all the faults of men.

LINES FOR CHRISTMAS CARDS.

SYMBOL'D by a tiny flower,
　　See my Christmas greetings sent ;
I remember thee this hour ;
　　Think of me, and I'm content.

Forget thee ! Life's joys are so mingled with sorrow,
　　Bitter and sweet are so mixed in the cup,
Little we guess what's in store for to-morrow,
　　Woes we may gain or delights render up.
Nay ; in the midst of this coming and going,
　　Ebbing and flowing of Time's changeful sea,
Oh ! there is comfort, real comfort in knowing,
　　I can find friendship unchanging in thee !

Make the best of everything,
Tho' 'tis often trying;
If you've spent your time in vain,
Waste no more in sighing:
Troubles may be manifold;
Keep a cheery heart and bold;
What's the use of crying!

What shall I wish my friend this Christmastide?
I'll wish twelve months of busy, joyous hours,
O'er which the thoughts that retrospective glide
Be but as sighs breathed over faded flowers.

MATERNAL LOVE.

POETS may sing of lovers' love,
   And tune the ancient lyre
To ceaseless rounds of plaintive song,
   Whereof men never tire !

A rarer subject, bolder I,
   My votive numbers move,
To sing in soft soliloquy
   A mother's tender love !

A mother's heart ! Oh, who can know
   The depths unfathomed there :
Depths far too sanctified to show
   The treasures none may share.

A mother's heart !—forgive me mine
　For that I dare to hope
My filial breast may half divine
　Some measure of its scope.

Maternal love begins to spring
　None knoweth how or when ;
But when maternal *cares* begin
　Maternal love *is* then.

Then what a happy doting stage
　In anxious love creeps by,
Until the sweetest, childhood age,
　Has joined eternity.

Boyhood succeeds ; oh, mother's heart,
　A trying time for thee ;
Keen pangs and many a bitter smart
　Are now thy destiny !

How anxious is the parent bird
　When, on its new-found wings,
The nestling first essays to try
　The strength its nature brings.

Who knows but that some wanton shot
   May check its quivering flight ;
Some snare embroil its guileless feet,
   Or pounce on it some kite ?

Divided in her anxious mind
   The old bird flutters by—
Fear for the little fledgling's flight,
   And joy that it can fly.

'Tis thus a mother's yearning fears
   Hover around her boy,
When first he leaves the sheltering nest
   To enter life's employ.

Yet was it not for this, for this
   Her tender, nurturing care
Had trained his pliant infancy
   And hallowed him with prayer ?

The time has come, and he must taste
   The tree of knowledge, too,
Must know 'twixt good and ill to choose—
   But which will he pursue ?

O do not slight a mother's love,
   Or think it "common-place";
The world knows no affection more
   Majestic or less base.

Death cannot slay a mother's love,
   It overleaps the tomb;
And to its object snatched away
   Bursts thro' the encircling gloom.

Forgotten words, forgotten deeds,
   Forgotten ways and looks,
Forgot by all but mother's heart,
   Are treasured in its nooks.

And oft—*how* oft she only knows,
   A mother's self bereaved—
Over the promise-breaking past
   Her lonely sighs are heaved.

And tho' the callous calls of life
   Forbid such pleasant pain,
Her thoughts a moment left alone
   Will flutter back again.

Night after night her spirit sleeps
  Upon some far-off grave;
While ever round her chilly sweeps
  Wild Fancy's phantom wave.

How oft to some light-spoken word,
  Or look, or touch, or sound,
The stricken heart-chords all vibrate
  And quivering rebound !

Shame, tenfold shame that sons should be
  To mock such tenderness,
And turn to curses on themselves
  A love that will but bless.

O mother's love, O love divine,
  Unselfish, constant, free,
How can thy sunbeams strike my soul
  And not reflected be ?

YOU'RE ANOTHER.

I LAUGH at thee,
You laugh at me,
We both laugh at our brother ;
He laughs at us both,
And neither is loth
To join his laugh at t'other !

A GREETING.

ABCDEFGHIJKLMNOPQRSTUVWXYZ.

I HAVE no special wish to tell—
   I wish you all and every good ;
So write the alphabet to spell
   Whene'er you will whate'er you would !

POETRY.

WHY do I read poetry ?
Everything is poetry :
Those who have but eyes to see
Find in all things poetry.
Why read books of measured rhyme
While all Nature is sublime
Unbefettered poetry ?
Sunset sky and evening star
Tell more thrilling poems far
To the hearts of listening men
Than was ever writ by pen ;
All is full of poetry :
Tinkling of the sheepfold bell,
Twinkling glowworms in the dell,
Sprinkling dews on heathery fell—
All is full of poetry.

Lying on the flowery grass
Watching swallows flickering by,
While the trailing cloudlets pass
In a variegated sky ;
Listening to the rippling stream
Prattling on its seaward way,
While the nodding rushes seem
Pleased with what the waters say—
What is this but poetry ?
Cataracts that loudly roaring
O'er the crags their deluge pouring
Lash the pools to tiny billows
Sputtering round the solemn willows,
Are heroic poetry.
Poetry in every measure
For all moods of grief or pleasure,
Nature keeps among her treasure.
Oh ! we need no books to read it,
All we need is eyes to heed it.
He that loved to say that poet
Was a synonym for " maker "
Libelled nature, tho' I know it,
Loved that lusty idol-breaker.
" Μουσῶν," said the Greeks, " προφῆται,"

Definition more complete I
Can't desire : for the muses
Are but Nature's several voices,
Which at various times she uses,
Whispering those on whom her choice is.
Poets do not make, they merely
Write at Nature's own dictation
For the deaf who cannot clearly
Apprehend her intonation :
To the blind the poet sings
All the myriad mystic things
'Neath the veil of Nature latent
To his clearer eyesight patent ;
He who hears the silent voices
Thrilling thro' his soul, rejoices
If he can but give expression
To one word of their confession.
He that hears the music soundless
Echoing thro' his spirit, tries
From a harmony so boundless
Just to seize, before it dies,
Here a bar, and here a line
Of a concert so divine ;
Hearing write, and written show it

To the world, which names him " poet."
Ah ! no poet ever sings us
Half the message Nature brings us,
Half the smiling springtime glories,
Half-stern winter's kindly stories ;
Never sings us, paints us, spells us,
Half each cycling season tells us :
Ne'er reflects one-half the light
That has made his own soul bright.
Words are feeble ; men are weak ;
Only half who feel can speak,
Less than half who speak can show
Nearly half of that they know.
All is full of poetry.
If you seek good poetry,
Leave the house and shut your book up,
Wander thro' the fields and look up ;
Look behind, before, about you,
Look within and look without you—
Look and listen ; listen gently,
Look not hardly but intently :
Thus you'll hear, and thus you'll see
Wheresoever you may be—
On the mountains, by the sea,

In the city's squalid gloom,
'Mid sweet dells of heath and broom,
In the garden, in the park,
In broad daylight, after dark,
Anywhere, at every time,
Poems, music, more sublime
Than was ever writ in rhyme,
Or than any could rehearse,
Or has prisoned in blank-verse ;
Try, and you will sing with me
All is full of poetry,
Everything is poetry.

THE LOSS OF THE *VICTORIA*.

THE Spirit of War was sporting
On the surging, sunlit sea,
As he scattered the scampering waters
In rollicking, reckless glee.

In the stately pomp of battle
He strode o'er the crested waves,
Who bow their proud heads,
As he lightly treads
O'er myriad nameless graves.

Then a war dance wild and weird,
He is mazed in a frenzied rage,
And he gloats o'er the glories attained in the past,
The trophies of every age.

His gorgeous bravery flits,
In the peace-breathing breeze from the shore,
As he whirls in a dazed, delirious delight,
In a dream of fresh glories in store.

O terrible Spirit of War !
O terrible even in play !
For you claimed for your sport
More lives than were sought
For a Roman Holiday.

Our brothers, husbands, sons,
Their life-blood spilled in vain ;
Not in the din of a foeman's guns,
They sank in a blood-stained main.

O what did you win ?   Nought !   Nought !
No records for history's pen ;
Applause of no people or court,
No heroes to add amongst men.

No heroes ?   Ah yes, they were there
But in death not in life they were proved;
For you strangled them e'er they could share
The contests you taught them to love.

Far down 'neath the gurgling deep,
Lie the stern sons of duty, thy slain ;
And the nations they cheer not, but weep,
And sympathy trembles with pain.

Yet had you not wrought this in play,
In such an unfortunate way,
But in grim earnest purpose intent—
Had you marshalled your troops,
'Mid yelling war-whoops,
On vengeance or plundering bent :
Had the roar of your thundering shaken
The walls of an alien town :
Had you clattered her stones
On enemies' bones
Mid hell-fire rattling down :
Had your sulphurous smoky pall
Drooped over the death-doomed site,
Where the blood of the dying and dead
Steamed up in the murky light ;
Where groans are lost in the roar that sped
The whistling cannon ball ;
The nation would view it with sparkling eyes,
And roar its delight to the echoing skies—
" Hurrah ! for the city is taken ! "

Had you foundered an enemy's ship,
And throttled a thousand men,
Your hand had been wrung in a friendly grip,

You had worn fresh laurels then !
Those mouldering forms 'neath the sea
Would be titles to honour, each one;
And all would an exquisite monument be
Of the glorious victory won !

O God ! is this our creed ?
Does brotherhood mean no more
For us than a common lust of greed
On a common native shore ?

O when shall we toss aside
This envy of race and clan,
And limit our " brothers " to nought less wide
Than the common rights of man ?

O God ! we are dull to learn ;
We are fools and slow of heart ;
And yet I wot we often yearn
To play a nobler part !

Can man *be* and not fight ?
But he was not born for this !
Is war his paragon bliss ?—
More light, my God, more light !

"DE AMICITIÂ."

CRUEL is the thought that the friends I am loving,
   Friends I have loved in the years passed away,
May in the future whereto we are moving
   Meet me a stranger as strangers some day !

Friends that I meet with, and laugh with, and talk
     with,
   Open my mind with, familiar and true,
Meeting again one that now I so walk with,
   Such should bow stiffly and say, " How d'ye do ? "

Yet, looking back on the past, I see clearly
   Shadows of friends I'm in touch with no more ;
Friends long ago that I loved very dearly
   Who have forgot the affection I bore.

I can see back through life's pathway in fancies
   Many a spot, where a hasty " Good-bye "
Left me without some companion, the chances
   Of some new bend in the roadway to try.

Shortly I joined some one else, and we started,
   Arm linked in arm a few miles on the way ;
Till we encountered more cross-roads and parted
   Almost before we could think what to say.

Yet, after all, 'tisn't friends that forsake us ;
   Friends, if worth keeping, will hold to us fast :
Ay, and the longer they stay, they will make us
   Love them the more for the love of the past.

Passing acquaintances we can dispense with ;
   We may have liked them or loved them, no doubt ;
But they were people we seldom talked sense with ;
   We feel their loss, but can manage without.

Just as a traveller, missing the pleasures
   Of a companionship lasting a week,
Soon from the midst of more durable treasures
   Can of his loss quite emotionless speak.

What is there dearer than friendship restraintless ?
  Should it wane, moon-like, each year that it lives ?
Love that is real, unaffected, and paintless—
  Ought it to feel any chill that time gives ?

No ! I don't fear any backbiting schemers,
  Envy, or other, co-partners in crime ;
They may yell under their draggling streamers ;
  The only real foe I'm in dread of is Time.

Friends I have loved in the past and am loving,
  Friends who to me are now loyal and true,
Say, when we meet whither now we are moving,
  Will ye bow stiffly and say, " How d'ye do ? "

ANALOGUE.

HEARTS are like the tent that Moses
Pitches for the Lord in Zin;
Where the outer wall encloses
Space that all may enter in.

Then a court for Israel's nation;
Last, the holiest of all,
Where one yearly makes oblation
At the stated season's call.

So with us; the outer veiling
Of our nature may be pass'd
By the many: but the second
By a few: by none the last.

There alone the spirit pleading
Stands before the mercy-seat;
Seeking strength for all its needing,
For the claims it fails to meet!

TO ALL WHOM IT MAY CONCERN.

YES ; you have suffered, none denies ;
    But now a truce to weeping.
Why, what's the use of all these sighs,
    And all this vigil-keeping ?

Come, plunge into the teeming world
    And bear your part in action ;
The work will bring a joy you'll find,
    To cure your soul's distraction !

We've something else to do below
    Than mourn the petty causes
Of all our woes ; our hurried lives
    ' Can't spare such lengthy pauses.

Pent in his narrow bounds of flesh,
    Six feet or so in stature,
Each deems his microcosmic sphere
    Is half the realm of Nature !

And thus he hugs his petty gains
  And mourns his trivial crosses,
As if the universe itself
  Were partner in his losses.

Go, count the stars, deluded fool !
  How many worlds gyrating
Around how many suns, and what
  Their speculated dating ?

Is this too much for heart and brain ?
  Then scale some City Steeple,
Or, say, the London Monument,
  And count the crawling people.

The swarming herds of men below,
  Like insect armies creeping,
With your self-bounded views of life
  Are strangely out of keeping.

Learn that the secret bands which knit
  Your life in that relation,
Which binds all units into one
  Vast Cosmos of creation,

Are rooted in the deeps below
    The glistening surface bubbles
Which swell, and flash, and fly, and burst,
    And fill your heart with troubles.

ALAS! A LOSS! AND A LASS!

WHERE the rocks run out to meet the hustling billows
    on the strand,
Where the ever-present gum-tree drives gnarled feet
    beneath the sand :

Stretching out gaunt arms to seaward, owning with a
    meagre grace,
Haughty deference to Nature, who forbids to claim
    that space.

Stretched upon a sea-worn block, among the boulders
    on the lea
Lie two human forms enveloped in a rug and reverie ;

In a peaceful meditation, cruising round the coasts of
    sleep,
Tuning pensive thoughts to rhythm with the pulses
    of the deep :

Gliding far away in spirit, leave their bodies on the
    shore,

Beckon old familiar friends and haunt the dreamy
    scenes of yore.

But a creaking on the shingle—is it fancy?—no,
    again !

Nearer, listen, creaking, creeping—something coming,
    that is plain.

What ?—a snake ? some vicious monster ? One form
    rises on an arm,

Then the other, see them, turning, eye the causes of
    alarm.

Fell the query from the spectre, " Are you going to
    bathe ? if not

We are, if you'll have the kindness to remove beyond
    this spot."

So we learnt 'twas maiden footsteps that alarmed our
    reverie,

And we rose in grim obedience to the laws of
    chivalry.

Vos valete !   O ! puellæ ; tho' you counterplayed
    our will,
Yet we joy to find such simple unaffected girlhood
    still.

And we'd sacrifice not only midday slumbers now
    and then,
Could we multiply such proofs to reassure despond-
    ing men.

SURSUM CORDA.

I FAIN would sing to a humble heart the song of a
    trustful hope ;
And what care I if others part the prize of a world's
    applause !
The cultured crowd in the covered stands, the mob
    that seethes at the rope,
May munch their sandwiches, clap their hands, or
    swear till the night give pause.

The air is thick with the noisy din of the rush and
    the scuffle of life,
And many are trampled by those who win a higher
    place than they ;
Till the cry goes up from the weary earth, from out
    the maddening strife,
That death is better for man than birth, and progress
    is but decay.

But I shout, " O man in the dust, take heart ! do all
    you can, and die ;

Nor fear that dying you miss your part ; fulfilment is
    elsewhere ;

For who can gauge success but He who knows all
    reasons why ?

Be faithful, let the issues be:" I cry, but who will
    hear ?

NOTA BENE.

SHE had sold her soul for bread—
Her soul for her body's life;
But the life she had bought was a living death,
So she buried its shame by a plunge beneath,
And a moment's drowning strife :
And Heaven shall judge the dead.

He had sold his soul for bread—
His soul for his stomach's lust ;
And the life he had bought was pampered and gay,
So he scribbled men's virtue and honour away,
A journalist traitor to trust :
And Heaven shall judge what he said.

CHRIST IN MODERN THEOLOGY.

STROPHE.

TAKEN away my Lord, and I know not where they
  have laid Him !

Taken away my life, and quenched the light of my
  spirit !

Life !—it was only to sit at the tomb of my blessed
  Redeemer ;

Only to mark where His feet had trodden the ways
  of the city ;

Only to dwell in the words the lips of my Saviour
  had spoken ;

Only to visit His grave with spices and flowers at
  daybreak.

There at the evening to kneel and pour out my spirit
  within me ;

Thence to go forth thro' the world to carry the balm
  of His teaching ;

Succouring those that He loved and whispering
  words He had uttered.

Him they have taken away, the Mainspring of all
  my existence ;

Him they have taken away, and I know not where
  they have laid Him.

Dark, dark is my life, I tremble to move in the darkness ;

Dark, darker is death, and eternity yawns to engulph
  me ;

Fathomless, drear, and too vast for the thought of a
  quivering mortal ;

Everywhere empty and dark and barren its depth
  and its vastness.

Ah ! the ineffable horror, the dread of that limitless
  vastness ;

Horror that broods in the gulph of that deep unlimited darkness.

He, the light of my life and the light of my death is
  departed ;

Him they have taken away, and I know not where
  they have laid Him,—

Taken my Master away, and I know not where they
  have laid Him.

ANTISTROPHE.

Wherefore seekest thou here among the dead for the
living?

Hearken, He is not here ! He is not here ! He is
risen !

Weep not thou for the dead, but joy and rejoice for
the living.

Rise, arise from the tomb, the empty tomb that they
made Him.

Here they thought to have kept His body for ever
imprisoned ;

Here, in the narrow cell that human chisels had
fashioned,

Would they have kept Him confined and honoured
Him after their manner.

Therefore rolled they a stone exceeding great on the
portal,

Therefore sealed it with seals by the hand of the
fathers and elders.

Him, the Lord of all life, they thought to enchain
with a signet,

Him with a boulder of rock they fondly conceived to
imprison.

Gone is the boulder of rock and broken the seals of
    the elders.
Seek not here 'mid the dead ; He is not here, He is
    risen.

STROPHE.

Who as speaking in dreams deceives with the cry,
    " He is risen " ?
Him they have taken away, and I know not where
    they have laid Him !
Taken away my Lord, and I know not where they
    have laid Him !

ANTISTROPHE.

Up and begone from the tomb, and go to tell His
    disciples,
Tell that He is not here ! He is not here, He is
    risen !
Rise and follow Him forth, and see Him and hear
    Him and ponder,
Not on the words that He spake before He was
    murdered and buried,
Not upon these alone, but also on those He is
    speaking ;

Not on the works that He wrought before His
    betrayal by Judas,

Not upon these alone, but also on those He is
    working :

Slow of heart to believe He is not here, He is risen !

PER CRUCEM AD LUCEM.

WERE body's good our highest good,
Then pleasure were our guiding star,
And sense true index of its course ;
But we have also souls whereby
We are communicant with God ;
In Him consists our highest good.
True Spirit of our spirit, Him
We are unswervingly to love ;
Not blindly, with instinctive drift ;
But freely, with clear inward sight
And conscious interchange of thought.
To this no antecedent wave
Of nervous feeling draws by sense
Of pleasure ; but, defying pain,
We reach pure joy unknown to sense,
And win our true inheritance.

A SIGH OF THE UNEMPLOYED.

THE past cut off and the future blank,
The present lonely, waiting ;
Waiting, ill, fallen out of the rank,
Waiting, empty in pocket and bank,
Expense accelerating !

Happy, happy days that are gone ;
Happiness—bitterness also :
They have departed, one by one,
Bitter and sweet they have left me none,
Ill and alone !—to fall so !

Ill and alone in the midst of a crowd,
Money nearly departed ;
Borrow or beg ?   Am I too proud
To blazon my helplessness out so loud ?
Work ! give work ! if work's allow'd !
O ! I am weary-hearted !

Work flows by in a given stream
Some can reach it only ;

Others stand by to shout and scream,
Wander about in an aimless dream,
"Out of the running"; so I seem,
Hankering and lonely.

Waiting like the man at the pool;
Angel troubles the waters;
In steps another—that's the rule,
One at a time—so I, poor fool,
Lie down again in Patience's school
With Misery's sons and daughters!

"Lord, I have no man," so he spake,
"By whom to be directed;
Others have friends whose hand they take
To lift them into the healing lake,
But I, so soon as the waters wake,
In going am intersected."

Courage! courage! desponding man;
Darker days have broken;
Cease the book of the fates to scan,
Banish to-morrows out of your plan,
To-day with enough for to-day began;
The past shall be your token!

MORS JANUA VITÆ.

O Parrot ! flashing in the sun,
  Whose life is but a toy,
A sportive wheel of radiant fun
  All circumscribed with joy,
For you a hundred years may run,
  While I must die a boy !

O Parrot ! with but half your days
  What might I do and be ;
While you will flutter in the sprays
  Of this and yonder tree,
And scream and twitter in the praise
  Of long inanity !

O Parrot ! flashing in the sun,
  I envy not, not I,
The days so lavished on your fun
  God's laws to me deny ;
For you a hundred years may run,
  But I shall never die !

TO ALTHEA.

O ! LOVE may often painful be
  A mockery of pleasure,
When lavished unreservedly
  In unbegrudging measure,
On one who deems such tribute vain,
And merely flings it back again,

           My Allie !

O ! love is full of life and hope,
  All interfused with pleasure,
Where he can find the fullest scope
  To spread his growing treasure ;
And ever richer grows and still
More rich the more remains to fill,

           My Allie !

O ! love must take as well as give,
   And gives the more for taking ;
Love hungers, but he cannot live
   On simpers and phrase-making ;
O ! love can live on scanty fare,
But thrives not when the table's bare,
           My Allie !

O ! love is mine, and mine is thine,
   For you and I, we tally,
And there is nothing so divine
   On earth as love, my Allie !
We'll give and take, and give the more,
And thus grow richer than before,
           My Allie !

'ΑΠΟΚΑΡΑΔΟΚΙΑ.

At times upon my soul there gleams
A glimmer as of rising day ;
And through the lessening darkness beams
Of flickering sunlight slope their way ;
And I, lone watcher of the night,
Shout, straining dawnwards weary sight,
    " The Light ! the Light ! "—but it is gone !

At times a spirit moves among
The dead bones of my common themes,
Wakes them to life—and I am stung
With shame of all my aimless dreams :
I watch each gathering to his post,
And cry, as one who finds the lost,
    " My Host ! my Host ! "—but they are gone !

At times I hear a voice within,
In tones my spirit leaps to hear ;
And hushed are all the sounds that win
The usual audience of mine ear ;
While every throbbing sense is strained,
I trembling whisper, pleasure-pained,
   " The Truth ! the Truth ! "—but it is gone !

O ! weary soul, the Day shall rise ;
The Hosts of God shall triumph still ;
Truth shall be clear as summer skies,
And Flesh to Spirit yield its will ;
Fear not ! be faithful to thy part,
'Tis all concerns thee ;—cries my heart,
   "My Hopes ! my Hopes !—they are not gone."

LOST AND FOUND.

THE SONG OF A MAIDEN ALL FORLORN.

I LOST my heart, I know not when,
 And wandered heartless weary days
 To blame inured, unknown to praise,
Amid the lives of fellow men,
A homeless stranger-citizen.

My careless comrades called me proud
 And cold and stiff ; and turned aside
 To criticise the latest bride
And sift the gossip of the crowd
With empty jest, and laughter loud.

From face to face I sought in vain
 For latent friendship's waking glance ;
 And if to theatre or dance
I went, return was always pain ;
Nor friend nor interest did I gain.

I lived an alien to their joys,
    A partner only in their grief ;
    While all my own, past all relief
They scoffed at, glorying in the toys
That please such grown-up girls and boys.

And thus my heart was ground away,
    And died myself, myself within ;
    Till all the clamour and the din
Of quarrels, merriment, display,
Passed heedless by me, day by day !

Until a voice within me spoke
    In tones my spirit heard and leapt
    From out the chamber where she slept ;
And all the spells of habit broke,
Before affection's master-stroke !

No longer now I live alone ;
    Strength is increased with fellowship ;
    Love smoothed the hardness from my lip
And turned my voice to purer tone ;
For in your heart I found my own !

THE IDEAL AND THE ACTUAL.

You tell me that one's character is known
   In choice of books their number and their kind ;
And thus conclude that mine is clearly shown,
   By these few various volumes that you find !

You say his garments are an index clear
   To any man's innate good taste or bad ;
And you would judge me by the clothes I wear,
   And label me with some one else's fad !

You view a man's companions and you pass
   Your inward judgment on his spirit's height ;
And judging thus you ticket me an ass,
   Because my comrades are so coarse and light !

If by his flight an eagle's strength you'd gauge,
   Or by his leap wouldst mete the kangaroo ;
You peer but idly in the cramping cage—
   Fling wide the barriers and let them go !

EPIGRAM.

'TIS said, " When soothsayers meet they smile " ;
  But when two sages meet they weep ;
For men pay any price for guile,
  But buy their wisdom " on the cheap ! "

TO R. W. EMERSON.

Good Friend, whose voice hath spurred and cheered
  My flagging spirit on its way ;
When, like a wilderness appeared
  My life to stretch a boundless grey
  And barren landscape to the day ;

When weakness raised its bitter cry
  For help, unheard of kith or kin ;
And sank in voiceless agony
  Beneath the load of others' sin
  Thy whisper reached it, " Look within ! "

How oft the rocks, beneath thy rod,
  Their streams of quickening hope have shed,
Where fainting hearts drank deep and trod,
  With strength renewed, where Duty led ;
  And Faith restored gleaned heavenly bread !

Good Friend ! if few have paused to bless
  For help received the helping hand ;
Accept as theirs than mine no less
  A stranger's tribute scratched in sand
  Upon a dry and thirsty land !

SICK-LISTED.

Ha! my friend, so we are comrades in the Red
  Cross tents of life,
Wounded each by wandering missiles in the maniac
  battle-strife ;
Well, a fig for all that turmoil! and a fig for all that
  din !
Let them stew in smoke and carnage ; what care I
  which side may win !
We'll be pensioned off as wounded ; and our days
  to ease may give.
How say you, my wounded messmate ?—Is it not
  enough to live ?

But I turned my aching temples from his vacant
  sordid stare,
And my scanty pulses swelling, throbbed to heaven
  in voiceless prayer ;

For my soul was longing, burning, to be out amongst
    the foe,
Cheering on my faltering comrades, parrying thrust
    and dealing blow !
All my eager spirit panted for the wildest of the fray,
For the place where I was fighting when I fell and
    swooned away.

And to hear this skulking scoundrel bless his soul
    that he was spared—
Spared for what ?—to swill his belly at his ease, who
    never cared
Aught for cause or aught for service, aught for aught
    but food and pay,—
Just to hear this base-born hireling bid me be con-
    tent to stay,
Nodding in a pensioned sunshine years that others
    give to strife—
Thus this sordid cur-souled creature bids me be
    content with life !

No ! my heart is in the battle ! It is marching with
    the flag ;
It is cheering on the valiant, it is rallying those who
    lag !

And it shouts with those whose voices rend the clouds
  with cries of hope ;
It is charging thro' the trenches ; rushing up the
  fortress-slope ;
Ever foremost of the foremost, it is pressing thro'
  the strife,
While I lie and hear this traitor chuckling o'er his
  scheme of life !

If I must resign my weapons, if I cannot fight again,
Not with self-congratulation, but with bitterest pangs
  of pain,
I will lay them on the altar in the temple of my
  God,
Where I girded them upon me e'er the battle-field
  I trod ;
And I'll stand among the servants arming warriors
  for the strife,
And invoking all their courage till they glow with
  half my life !

TO V. F. S.

A DIVER from the murky bed
   Of life's dark ocean, hails the care
   Of him above who pumps the air
Adown the pipe whence life is fed.

Good friend, who in the upper light
   Canst draw free breath and scan glad skies,
   Not thoughtless of the toil which plies
Where one dim lantern copes with night,

I thank thee.   Sitting far remote
   I keep thee near by mutual signs ;
   And from the straining of the lines
I learn the tossing of thy boat.

I, seeking pearls, find empty shells
    And tangled weed and barren stones,
    And stumble over dead men's bones
And wrecks of ancient diving-bells.

Thy senses roam at liberty
    Thro' scenes that I would gladly know ;
    Yet I have seen strange things below
And wonders only divers see !

Thy labour brings its daily prize ;
    I little gain with much ado ;
    But if I find a pearl or two
I'll share them with thee, when I rise.

Condemn not that its metre lends
    My verse its beauty, since I sought
    To wake an echo in the thought
Of him whose friendship made us friends !

FROM "THE ORDER OF THE BEAN."

(Specially inspired by the ghost of an idea of antique etymological aspect.)

PERCHĀNCE this serious trifle, borne
    Of couplit thought and spritelie iest,
Maye gayne thȳe eare, and clepe thy scorne
    On al yᵉ follies yᵗ infeste
    Ovre lyttle lyves, yᵉ vvorste, yᵉ beste.

Bot, an it preve off power to drawe
    To larger loue, to wyder thought
For Beavtie in yᵉ formes of Lawe—
    For Lawe as Heauen, not Costome, taught,
    Not whollie is myne Travayle nought !

Still miscōtente, I fai would se
    In hem who stryue, ne stryue in vayne,
Mo' mockle-hearted charitee
    Toward those who ever fayle agayne ;
    For Oh ! yᵉ worlde ben farsed wid payne !

THE ORDER OF MELCHIZEDEC.

A MOUNTAIN and a multitude that climb :
A deep, dense mass of upward striving men,
Led by a band of heroes proved and loved
By all the following legions ; these again
By valiant leaders headed, this or that,
For he is leader for the time who leads.
These guide the course, and with their vanguard
      clear
Thro' rocks and thickets, over and around
All threatening barriers, roadway for the crowd
Of following pilgrims ; pressing restless on,
Upward and onward.   And I saw the men
Were sons of Science and Philosophy,
Broad-browed, dispassionate and purposeful.
But ever up the rugged steep a cry
Far from the rearward struggled to the front :
" We are your leaders, Pilgrims ; wait for us !"

Till he who led, unpausing, raised his voice :
" If ye indeed be leaders, come and lead !"
" Nay ; follow ye behind us !" moaned the voice.
Whereat the leader laughed a bitter laugh
Of angry sorrow ; crying to the rear,
" If ye be leaders, lead us, and we follow."
Then they whose clamorous protest broke the peace
Of all those striving myriads came in sight—
A band of clergy toiling at the heels
Of that procession, in the beaten track
Smoothed by the tramping of uncounted feet.
While some indeed, misliking not to lead,
Since powerless to lead upward, called upon
The multitudes to turn and follow down
The backward trail to old-time camping grounds ;
Yet ever from the vanguard rose the cry
Of men still striving upward ; and the cheer
That woke a thousand echoes greeted each
Discovery of new bypath, or the crash
Of battered rocks and falling forest trees.
And still the cry wailed ever, " Wait for us !"
While down the backward gorges whence it rose
The answer pealed, " If ye be leaders, lead !"

TO A " BLACK-FELLOW."

DIRT, disease, and degradation, seal you of a dying
   race ;
Dim despondency has graven reckless lust upon your
   face,
Where the play of transient feeling marks the range
   of appetite,
As the scowl of rage alternates with the leer of coarse
   delight.

We who boast an age of progress, prate of science,
   ethics, art,
Can we strike a single keynote that will vibrate in
   your heart ?
Have you aught in common with us that we share not
   with the beasts ?
Could you be a saint or hero if we gave you books
   and priests ?

Children we of common parents, infusoria and apes ;

You stagnated somewhat lower in the intermediate
   shapes

Of transition ; and we clambered, age by age, from
   high to higher,

Learnt to set the curb of reason in the jaws of wild
   desire.

But the white-skinned scoundrels, boasting birthright
   of a nobler name,

Have belied their higher nature, damned their souls
   in deeds of shame ;

While the cry of vanquished weakness claimed protection of the strong

They have swamped the plea for justice in a slough
   of hellish wrong !

In the sordid greed of plunder and the vileness of
   brute-lust

They have trampled half thy kindred in their out-
   raged native dust ;

Swept the shuddering remnant backward to the lairs
   · of dogs and swine,

Or degraded to the baseness of a nature such as thine.

Not a man of all these myriads, babbling of "superior
    right,"
Dares to plead for common justice 'twixt the black
    man and the white ;
Men of science with false logic soothe to sleep our
    conscience-qualms,
Preachers find excuses for us in the hexateuch and
    psalms.

Those who hold our England's audience jingle purses
    in her ear,
Feed her fancy with smooth phrases in set speeches
    year by year :
Who will scourge these shallow flatterers from her
    councils, with the cry
That shall wake her to do penance for her shameless
    perfidy ?

Thou—I care not if our Science bracket thee with
    wallabies,
If it teach he is but thwarting natural Law whoever
    tries
To protect the type that, aidless, must evaporate in
    death,
Let the God who made thee slay thee, I'll be guiltless
    of thy breath !

And if worthier champions fail thee, and all abler
  tongues are mute

At the clamorous bar of Justice I will plead your
  righteous suit ;

Thou and I are fellow-subjects, and the law which
  shelters me

Shall be thundered in defiance of the crimes which
  outlaw thee !

TO TENNYSON.

GREAT singer, we who hear thy song
　　Still resonant with timeless thought
Thro' life's dim highways press along
　　In clamorous crowds ; and there is nought
But memory of thy voice to cheer
Our faltering footsteps marching here !

New needs arise with every day,
　　And none is found to fill thy place,
To cheer us on the onward way,
　　As thou the past, with words of grace.
We miss the strong, deep-natured man
Who marched so bravely in our van.

Meanwhile a band of Pipers shrills
　　Thin airs to keep our feet in time ;

And weary heart with languor fills
  At jinglings of unmeaning rhyme,
Which wakes no echo in the skies
Where thrilled thy rolling symphonies.

We pipe resettings of thy notes,
  And little ditties of our own ;
And some have given reluctant votes
  To set another on thy throne ;
But none can crown Occasion's brow
With such a comely wreath as thou !

Our Poet ; dear to every heart
  Which found its utterance in thine own,
If thou canst hear us where thou art,
  And shudderest not through every bone,
From all these Pipers take, thro' me,
This tribute to thy memory !

A NEW LITTLE WOMAN.

SAID a winsome maid of eight—
Nothing could be prettier—
" Which do you the higher rate,
Longfellow or Whittier ? "

Swallowing down a mild surprise
I replied, " With deference
To your wishes, I surmise,
Madam, you've a preference ;

" And I beg you'll kindly say——"
" Yes," she blushed, " it's Whittier ! "
In her knowing little way—
Nothing could be prettier !

" I presume, then, that you know——"
" Blacksmith ? Yes ; and—bother it !
I forget its name, altho'
I have read another bit ! "

"AMOR DEI ET PROXIMI."

TO A. N. D.

To him who first upon his bloody shield
This legend of your ancient house engraved,
The love of neighbour meant the love of kin,
The love of nation and the love of friends.
Thus bearing thro' fierce times a zeal misled,
Dissundering God and friends, from devil and foes,
He thought he did God service with his sword.
But you have learnt the fatherhood of God
Unlimited by politics or creed ;
And in this wider sense of fatherhood
Have learnt a wider meaning in the term
Of neighbour'; and for generous acts, the fruit
Of large-souled kindness, take a neighbour's thanks !

HEINE'S GRAVE.

Man of sovereign worth was he,
Rich in all philanthropy;
Reverence marked him for her own,
And Religion called him son.
Full of gentle sympathy;
Rich in large-souled charity;
Ever serving humankind
With the products of his mind.
Pure in thought, in diction chaste;
Every noble impulse graced
Him whose fame can never die.
Here he lies—and so do I!

RELIGION.

Since God is All in All, and all things tend
To God and find their being in His life,
The laws of their relations with themselves
Have all their final reference to Himself.
And in this reference of all law to God
We metaphrase Religion ; and in this
That man should live conformably to law
And school rebellious passions into line
Is human duty.   All the lower forms
Of inorganic and organic life,
Unconscious of the goal to which they tend,
And serving blind sensation, worked the will,
Unconsciously, of Heaven ; till the dawn
Of that mysterious faculty whereby
From brutes rose men ; who, conscious of themselves,
And conscious of that other than themselves,

Spelt out the laws of Nature, and henceforth
Adjusted reasoned means to conscious ends.

The power of choice is ours : to sink in low,
Ignoble ends of self-aggrandisement ;
Or, rising to the fulness of our height
As free-born rulers, to subdue the world
Each in the sphere of his own influence,
To higher and to ever higher law ;
Till this material chaos be reduced,
From anarchy, confusion, and despair,
To symmetry, consistency, and peace !

DIALOGUE.

'ΑΙΣΘΗΣΙΣ

You see the toils these athletes undergo
In training for their contest, three weeks hence :
Methinks so much good labour is misspent
Upon such slight returns, such trivial ends !

ΔΟΞΑ.

Your shallow judgment misconstructs the theme
This spectacle should offer to your thought ;
You see but athletes training for their games ;—
Are they not soldiers toughening for war ?—
Statesmen, upstoring elements of strength ?—
Divines out-sweating morbid monkish thought ?—
Men who shall some day bear in wider spheres
A nobler part in action for the toil
You reprimand as squandered on their sport?

Deduct our athletes from the empire's roll
Of mighty men of valour, in those deeds
Which raised us to the headship of this globe
And wield the widening influence of our race,
And who is left ?

ΕΠΙΣΤΗΜΗ.

So far, I grant, so good ;
You pause too soon ; the trail of flitting thought
Perchance too slight to draw your flurried sense
To its last issue in that trackless waste
Of speculation, whence Experience turns
Her ever-baffled footsteps back to earth.
These athletes, training, as we see, for sport,
Are training, as you taught us, for an age
Of nobler purpose and more worthy ends.
But in the larger training-ground of life
I think of those at war with circumstance ;
Whose days consume in profitless attempt
To do what, done, were little in itself
To grace the doing ; ever bending vast
And well-concerted energies to cope
With some inevitable pettiness ;

All greatest qualities of heart and mind
Lavished on trifles, as spectators deem,
In some such shallow verdict as our friend's.
Are there not wider spheres for later days,
And nobler uses for such qualities ?
For spiritual muscle, so to say,
Is trained like his who yonder thumps that bag
Of senseless sand ; he trains for worthier foes,
Nor do we find life's issue in its close.

NATURAL LAW IN THE SPIRITUAL WORLD.

CASES of fruit, of quality and size
Most various, piled by hurrying crowds of men
In the broad entrance of a packing-house.
'Tis thus, me-thought, that Genius pours her wealth
Of learning, wisdom, and inventiveness
Upon the threshold of succeeding years.

The piling ceased ; and in the further halls
The hands of busy hundreds sort the fruit,
Range it in various classes, kind with kind ;
And all are tested by a practised skill
That noted every blemish, and the bad
Rejected. And I thought 'tis even so
With fruits of human wisdom : here a man
Pours all the contents of his ripened thought ;
And others sort it, criticise, compare,

Reject the bad and classify the good.

The men who bring the harvest from the fields,

Not these are they who scrutinise the load ;

Nor are the critics those most rich in thought ;

Nor yet an analytic epoch rich

In new inventions : but its work is vast.

SPRING.

(FROM THE GERMAN.)

WHEN the Springtime upward scales,
And in sunshine melts the snow,
Round the tree fresh greenery trails,
In the grass first flowerets glow:
> When pass away
> The dreary day
> And long, dull winter nights ;
> The heights proclaim
> To the valleys wide
> Thy wonderful name,
> O sweet Springtide !
When the ice the sunshine licks,
From the mount the streamlet springs,

With young green each object decks,
And with joy the forest rings :
    The flowering leas
    Perfume the breeze,
    And heaven smiles clear and blue ;
    The heights proclaim
    To the valleys wide
    Thy wonderful name,
    O sweet Springtide !

DE PROFUNDIS.

THIS solitude ! this solitude !   Oh, heart,
How long, how long unbreaking canst thou beat
Time to the leaden moments of these hours,
Which drag thro' sullen weeks and months unlit
By any joy of living, or by hope
Of any brightening prospect ?   Day by day
I nerve me to fresh effort, and again
Sink fainting 'neath the self-inflicted spur ;
While all my social nature cries for some
Strong word of human fellowship—in vain.
Alone I ride these dreary leagues of bush,
Alone I track the mountains, and alone
In pain and weakness lie long hungering days
Dazing a fevered brain with unshed tears ;
Or forcing mirthless laughter at forced thoughts
That simulate a spectral cheerfulness

From sense of duty, and relentless need
Of gayer moments to defeat despair.
Myself, myself !—I come to dread myself,
And too self-conscious shrink from thought of self,
And thro' too much familiarity
Have lost the clue to self-hood, being now
One man, now two ; not knowing which is I,
Which my companion *alter ego*, born
Of self-reflection—he whose image gleams
In horror at me from my looking-glass,
Reflecting mine own horror.   In mine ears,
Strained in the silence of this solitude,
I hear the whirring pulses as I sit
Alone, in this vast wilderness of trees ;
Snatching a glad relief in distant screams
Of fighting parrots ; or the choric laugh
Of Cuckooburroughs ;—sounds we set to thoughts
Of any burden of familiar moods,
Cheering the cheerful, saddening the sad.
This solitude ! this solitude !   Oh, heart,
Braced by the strength of mutual fellowship,
Thou too hast known the impulse of brave thought,
Nor from stern duties shrunk in other days.
But here—how long, unbreaking, canst thou beat

A muffled drum to actions void of use
That perish in the doing ?   I had friends
In summer hours, and in lesser need,
Whose merest word of confidence and love
Would pour new life thro' every scanty vein ;
But such words come not !   Otherwise there come
Cold hints of cruel suspicions and hard thoughts
That shame the name of friendship.   Of the rest
Scarce one who spends a casual postage-stamp
To ask how fares it with the absent one.
I have no heart to blame them ; and, please God,
If happier days shall ever dawn again,
I'll walk with them in sunshine, as before,
Who feared to walk in darkness with their friend.

DANTE.

GREAT Dante, hadst thou lived in Virgil's days
Thou hadst o'ertopped thy Virgil in the ranks
Of world-famed poets ; or in Milton's age,
Hadst rivalled our strong Milton ; but, as they
Who held Thought's mirror to the face of Time
Showed each the symptoms of his time's decay,
So thou, whose age was sickening unto death,
Showed Death's cachectic features in thy glass ;
And we who read there praise the poet's skill,
But loving not Death's features turn away !

WOMAN'S RIGHTS.

You wish you were a man, my dear,
  For men have wider lives,
And less restricted liberties,
  Than sisters, daughters, wives ?

And so you think a woman's life
  Too petty, narrow, small ;
Indeed, you hold a woman's life
  Is scarcely life at all.

I grant you, in the race for fun,
  Which sometimes is called life,
A youth or husband has more chance
  Than has a maid or wife.

But I would change a hundred men
  For one such girl as you ;
And I would fain my manhood held
  Your power's mystic clue.

Beyond the tasks of daily life,
  Beyond its outer show,
There is a joy for womanhood
  That manhood cannot know.

I saw you with that weeping girl
  Clasped gently to your breast ;
I saw you kiss her tears away,
  And soothe her heart to rest ;

I could but speak a kindly word,
  So commonplace ! so cold !
While you can share your very heart
  With her your arms enfold.

The world is full of saddened hearts
  No man has power to cheer ;
And for this gift of womanhood
  I envy you, my dear !

O cast no idle blame on Fate
  That you are not a man ;
But use a woman's privilege
  As only woman can !

THE SONG OF THE BILLY.

WE have no Pollies here to put the kettles on for tea ;
We have no kettles in this land of gum and wallaby ;
But we've strong hands and cheerful hearts ; the
    bread and mutton's good ;
And we've a Billy boiling on a pile of blazing wood.
      Hurrah ! then, for the Billy, boys,
      Hurrah ! hurrah ! hurrah !
      Let others prate of kettles, boys,
      We're better as we are !
      Australia for Australians ! and the Billy, boys,
        for me !
      Hurrah, boys, for the Billy ! and hurrah for
      Billy tea !

We live the life of Freemen in this country of the
    Free ;
We clear the path to empire for a nation yet to be :

It's not an easy life, you bet, to be a pioneer ;
It's not a bit romantic when you come to see it near.

> But the Billy cheers our spirits, boys,
> Hurrah ! hurrah ! hurrah !
> Let others prate of tea-pots, boys,
> We're better as we are !
> Australia for Australians ! and the Billy, boys,
>> for me !
> Hurrah, boys, for the Billy ! and hurrah for
>> Billy tea !

I own eternal living in an atmosphere of sheep,
Makes mutton rather wearisome and pastoral poems
    cheap ;
But a gallop after emus, or a mob of kangaroos,
Gives monotony the go-by, and is patent for " the
    blues."

> Hurrah ! then, for the Billy, boys,
> Hurrah ! hurrah ! hurrah !
> Let others prate of coffee-pots,
> We're better as we are !
> Australia for Australians ! and the Billy, boys,
>> for me !
> Hurrah, boys, for the Billy ! and hurrah for
>> Billy tea !

The're some of us are jackeroos, and some are swag-
men grey;

And some are boundary-riders, some troopers, some
survey;

Selectors, miners, pastoralists—whatever we may
be,

Our saddles carry Billies, and we swear by Billy
tea.

> Hurrah! then, for the Billy, boys,
>
> Hurrah! hurrah! hurrah!
>
> Let others prate of beer-jugs, boys,
>
> We're better as we are!
>
> Australia for Australians! and the Billy, boys,
> for me!
>
> Hurrah, boys, for the Billy! and hurrah for
> Billy tea!

EPITHALAMIUM.

SWEET Bride, on this your wedding-day,
 My heart rejoices in your bliss,
 And blesses you and him whose kiss
Has sealed what love has vowed away.

My gift is poor ; for scant my purse ;
 I have no gold, no pearls to send ;
 But what I have I freely spend
To buy this greeting strung in verse.

My gift is poor ; despise not such !
 Perchance the crowded tables bear
 No gift midst those that glisten there,
That cost the giver half so much !

AD VERECUNDIAM.

I CANNOT blame thee, oh ! my friend,
 I have no heart to chide ;
Remonstrance ?—Shall I plead with thee,
 And swallow down my pride ?

That pride which placed thee high above
 All rivals—far apart !
That pride which found an anchorage
 For faith within thy heart !

If all the years we lived and loved
 Convince not I am true,
Then go on hooting with the crowd
 I will not plead with you !

FEAR NOT, LITTLE FLOCK.

I GRANT you the world would revolve as before,
With little of difference to praise or deplore,
If the faith of the gospel were swept from its sky
And Time took no thought of an Eternity.
For the maxims of conduct, which govern the race,
Were never the maxims of Him they disgrace.

The man in the street, be he Christian or Turk,
Buddhist, Pagan, or Jew, he will live in his work;
And the god of his worship, whatever his creed,
Is the thing that will pander to sensuous need.

One man in ten thousand, perchance, may be known,
Who lives by the faith he professes to own :
But not all the wisdom of Science can say
The worth of that man in the world of his day ;
And the worth of such men,—two or three, here and
    there,—
In the lapse of long ages, what sage will declare ?

JAMESON'S RIDE.

LET silly girls and hare-brained lads
  Applaud the plucky action ;
Thank Heaven, we are not ruled by " fads,"
  Or by caprice of faction :
A thousand interests clash and shake
Blind Reason with the din they make !

Let those bepraise such giants' play,
  Who lack what we are made of ;
We have a million brave as they
  Who are no Boers afraid of ;
Too brave, too noble, and too wise
To move till Duty bids them rise !

Let brigands through their country's shame
  Hew out a road to glory ;

But there are other roads to fame
   In our Old England's story ;
And men content to toil unknown
· Have spread the empire of her throne !

Let hare-brained lads and silly girls
   Applaud the shameful action ;
Thank Heaven, our judges shake their curls,
   At " personal attraction " ;
And reckless knights who ride too fast,
In " Black Maria " ride at last !

IN A SWISS CHURCHYARD.

A VILLAGE of one street ; and scattered huts
Upon the gently-climbing mountain slope ;
A hostel, and a school-house, and a church ;
A wind-wall of steep hill tops ; and afar
Low thunder of wild waters in the vale,
And rhythmic murmur of funereal pines.

A narrow life within a narrow sphere,
Some scores of souls wear daily towards its close ;
Like prisoned birds content to hop their cage,
And, ever hopping where they hopped before,
Conceiving of no ampler life than theirs ;
And, having seed and water, ask no more.

The village church, where he who preaches lends
The colour of his fancy to the thoughts
Of those who listen ; and the small churchyard,

Where he has laid their dead ; and with them made
The last still resting-place of one not theirs.
After long wanderings over weary years,
I come, sweet child, to greet your resting-place.
I knew you not while living here, nor knew
The scenes of your last daylight ; now, long dead,
I gather flowers on your little grave,
And lose you once again in thinking o'er
The distant days of sadness when you died,
And all the dream-like memories of your life !

Death ? I know not what is Death.
    Life ? what is it that departs
With the last expiring breath,
    And the throbbing of our hearts ?

Can a soulless body live ?
    No ; then bodies cannot die ;
And the spirit we believe
    Heir of immortality.

Matter is but gas condensed,
    And the loveliest human shape
May be otherwise dispensed,
    As the body of an ape.

Countless myriads of worms,
  Regimented and controlled
By a higher soul, that forms
  Them within its plastic mould,

Make the bodies which we have,
  Till at death the spirit's sway
Is withdrawn; and, in the grave,
  Back they go to worms and clay!

Matter in a given mass,
  Interfused with that which gives
Typal being, brings to pass
  Life in everything that lives!

Thro' all life's ascending course
  Matter, trained to use of soul,
Gains, at every death, new force
  For the service of the whole!

And the whole, as recomposed
  In new bodies brings a skill
Of expression to be used,
  Yet unknown, by living will.

Thus, the individual life
  Of the spirit in flesh-thrall,
By its ceaseless inward strife
  Ministers to that of all !

Yet, I find not in the flowers
  Which I gather on thy grave,
Any trace of higher powers
  Than more common grasses have !

Foolish protest ! Should one make,
  With a microscope and knife,
Search for forces which can wake
  Only in a human life ?

Thus of body : what of soul ?
  Is its future as its past ?
Does it live a conscious whole ?
  Or subserve a whole more vast ?

And of those who pass away
  In the spring-time of their life ;
Are we better off than they,
  Who are left to longer strife ?

Are they better off than we,
　　Called away while we fight here ?
Sons of immortality,
　　Can it matter, here or there ?

There is no death, but changing modes of life.
Then do we make that man responsible
To untold ages of eternity
For every soul he couples with the form
Of human body ? and does chance decide
By casual meetings of young men and maids
The type of an hereditary soul
That knows no dissolution like its dust ?
Or are all souls potentially alike
In power and goodness, limited by force
Of bodily inheritance till then,
When Death gives freer scope to each, elsewhere,
To move unfettered in a wider life ?
And she, the sweet young sister buried here—
Are we but Chance's debtors that she lived ?
Or was the freedom of her parents mocked
By fixed decrees of Heaven ?   Then the sin
Which placed a Norman monarch on our throne
And tinged our dynasties with Tanner's blood

Was sinless, being helpless. Whence souls
    come,
And with what stamp of character; or how
Befettered by ancestral sinfulness,
It boots us not to question : that they live
In consciousness of duty and in hope
Of higher service, will suffice to guide
Our life's brief action, knowing Whom we serve.

Dear child, whom we, while year succeeds to
    year,
Miss ever from our lives, our hearts, our home,
We laid thy weary body down to rest
In this lone grave among the Rhetian Alps ;
And with thee buried all we knew of life,
Of death, of this world and the next, save this
That our blind souls bear witness to a hope
Which baffles words' expression ; and we trust
That He who gave the love which mourns thy
    loss
Will give that love fulfilment : thus farewell !

DAVOS LAKE.

REST—rest in peace!—the last strong prayer of
  faith,
Wherewith we lay our loved ones down to sleep
Their last long sleep in death's dark, narrow bed.
Rest—rest in peace! aye, peace is for the dead ;—
Who knows? perchance new conflicts meet the
  soul
Beyond the portals of its earthly life.
Peace—rest and peace! Who is it sighs for
  peace ?
Who dreams a blank eternity of rest ?
Rest is a means to labour, not its end.
But there are restful labours, weary heart.
Yea, I am weary of a ceaseless strife—
Within—without ;—here will I rest in peace,
Here, on the margin of a mountain lake,

Among dark pines and many-flowered grass,
Here still the echoes of those jangling notes
Which vibrate from the haunts of fellow-men.
Here for a moment will I rest in peace.
There is a power in Nature like to hers
Whose touch and word could soothe the fluttering
    pulse
Of first conflicting passions : less perhaps
This power is a semblance than the same ;
For Nature is the mother of us all.
The gentle plashing of this mountain lake,
The play of sunlight on its mimic waves, ·
The rustling of the larches in the breeze,
The chirping of young sparrows overhead—
These calm to rest.   Do these, then, rest in
    peace ?
No ; all is active where all seems so still.
The very beetle crawling through the grass
Works out some scheme of beetle hope or fear,
Works out some larger purpose than he knows ;
Those scintillating sunbeams on the lake,
That seem ensymboled freedom of delight,
Are drawing water skywards. Strange that all
Work with delight and find such joy in work,

While man, the noblest, does despite to joy
In following duty !   There be some who teach
All joy is duty ; some, all duty joy.
God grant—I pray my blessing curse them not—
God grant them joyful duties ! but, for me,
I pray new strength for duties void of joy !

O clear, deep, plashing waters of the lake !
Folk say your depths are soundless ; and therein
I bury all the restless, fretful thoughts
That drove me weary to your sylvan banks.

Beyond the lake the Shiahorn and the Berg
Of Dörfli, and the ragged cliffs erstwhile
Rough-hewn by glaciers.   Why do all men love
To gaze on mountains ?   Cramped in little spheres,
Where little acts wear out their little lives,
They love the mountains for their very size,
And read a fuller meaning into life
From those huge, mystic symbols of a time
And space unbounded by the wonted course
Of daily nothings that employ their souls.
We need such special symbols, like a child
Who needs *italics*, CAPITALS, and marks

Of exclamation in his lesson-book
To emphasise the phrases.   Slow of heart !
There's not a pebble in the crowded street
But antedates the Pharaohs ; not a star
But saw the building of those mountains there,
And soon will see them crumble ; for the hills
Are but as earth-waves, and the earth itself
A passing meteor ; and the thoughts of God
Are graven in our science ; and we read,
Yet scorn to claim our birthright, bargaining still
For every mess of potage that we see,
And wrangling o'er them, like a mass of flies
That buzz and struggle in a honey-pot.
Here, stranded on the mountains, crippled lives
Creep to the grave, or struggle back to health
Thro' tedious years of hope deferred by hope.
Ambitions thwarted snarl themselves to sleep ;
And passions stayed from freedom vent mean spite
In petty malice ; and the practised strength
Of nobler spirits trained in earlier strife
Grows feeble fighting midgets.   Is such life
Worth living ?   Foolish doubt of faithless heart !
If life be but the destined path to goals
Of our own marking, then self-chosen aims

In failing thwart the purpose of our lives,
And death were our best wisdom.   But we live
To rear no cenotaph of toil-won gold,
To win no title to regard of men,
To do no deeds of generous-hearted strength,—
Else were all merit but a synonym
For opportunity ; we live to do
Each duty in its hour ; and, perchance,
If petty duties for their pettiness
Are harder doing than more worthy deeds,
There may be nobler Service in the faith
That shrinks not from them.   Thus reflection climbs
Through thoughts of human nature to the laws
Of that wide Nature wherein man has part,
And thence to Him, both man's and Nature's God,
In whom alone our souls can rest in peace.

UNWIN BROTHERS, THE GRESHAM PRESS, WOKING AND LONDON.

www.ingramcontent.com/pod-product-compliance
Lightning Source LLC
Chambersburg PA
CBHW020622030726
47497CB00007B/2372